Hickory Dickory Stalk

SUSAN ROGERS COOPER

AVON BOOKS  NEW YORK

VISIT OUR WEBSITE AT
http://AvonBooks.com

HICKORY DICKORY STALK is an original publication of Avon Books.
This work has never before appeared in book form. This work is a novel.
Any similarity to actual persons or events is purely coincidental.

AVON BOOKS
A division of
The Hearst Corporation
1350 Avenue of the Americas
New York, New York 10019

Copyright © 1996 by Susan Rogers Cooper
Published by arrangement with the author
Library of Congress Catalog Card Number: 96-96173
ISBN: 0-380-78155-7

First Avon Books Printing: October 1996

AVON TRADEMARK REG. U.S. PAT. OFF. AND IN OTHER COUNTRIES, MARCA REGIS-
TRADA, HECHO EN U.S.A.

Printed in the U.S.A.

RA 10 9 8 7 6 5 4 3 2 1

A DEADLY KISS

Megan was kneeling on the cobblestone patio. Blood was pouring from her mouth.

"Oh my God!" I knelt beside her. "Did you swallow any?"

She shook her head, her eyes huge.

"Spit!" I said. "Spit it all out!" I turned to my son. "Graham, call 911!" I shouted, trying to be heard over Bessie's screams. Bessie has a problem with blood. A problem that started when her birth family was murdered in her presence.

Graham ran in the house while I held my daughter and tried to see if all the glass and chocolate were out of her mouth. In less than a minute, Graham was back on the patio, the portable phone in his hand and the first tears I'd seen in his eyes since he broke his toe at age three.

"Mama," he said, "they told me to stop playing with the phone. They won't come!"

"A GUTSY NEW SLEUTH"
Kirkus Reviews

"SUSAN ROGERS COOPER IS A GIFTED
AND PERCEPTIVE WRITER
WHOSE CHARACTERS
ARE SECOND TO NONE."
Sharyn McCrumb, author of
The Hangman's Beautiful Daughter

To my agent, Vicky Bijur,
for all you do, have done,
and will do

Acknowledgments

I would like to take this opportunity to thank my friend Judy Miller, better known as Judith Miller, MSW, CSW, for her helpful insight into the human condition, and my daughter Evin Cooper for picking the brains of her co-workers and superiors down at the Travis County Sheriff's Department.

As always, my grateful appreciation to the members of the Black Shoes—Jeff Abott, Jan Grape, and Barbara Burnett Smith—for their insights and critiques, and to my husband, Don Cooper, for practically the same thing, and so much more.

A very special thank you to my editor, Tom Colgan, for having faith in E.J. She and I both thank you.

One

I jumped a foot when someone knocked on the back door. Which was unfortunate, since I was holding a very full measuring cup of bleach at the time, which spilled all over a pair of size 9 slim junior jeans. I hoped tie-dyeing was back for good. I set the cup of bleach down on the washer and stepped over my two five-year-old daughters, who had picked the crowded laundry room in which to play. I landed squarely on Ernie's tail. He screamed, which sent Bert into a small seizure (he does that) and both girls grabbed a leg each (mine). Axl Rose, third of the trio of cats, sat a distance away, disdainfully glaring at the melee out of his one good eye, while he lazily cleaned a pristine paw.

I shook and pulled my way into the breakfast room to the back door. Opening it against the cold March wind, I was greeted by a grunt of acknowledgment from sixteen-year-old Brad McLemore. At the sight of me, Brad turned a dark red, emphasizing the mountainous zit on the side of his jaw. Brad had a new haircut with shaved spots at both temples, leaving only a tuft of wheat-colored hair at the top. His corduroy shorts were four sizes too large and worn so low on the hips that the crotch was at his kneecaps and the hem of the shorts hit him mid-calf, an inch or two above his unlaced, dirty, high-top sneakers. The five sizes too large T-shirt sported a huge marijuana leaf on the front.

"Hi, Brad," I said, opening the door.

Speaking to him only made the boy turn a deeper shade of red. "I need to get Conner," he said.

I opened the door wider. "Sure," I said, "come on in." To my daughters, I said, "Run upstairs and tell Conner his brother's here."

Both girls ran off in a flash, which justified my suspicion that these bouts of "we grab mama by the leg because we love her so" behavior had more to do with boredom than insecurity.

"Would you like something to drink?" I asked Brad. "Soda? Juice?"

"You got a Coke?" he asked, following me into the kitchen.

I took out a can from the fridge and handed it to him, as I leaned against the counter. "So, how's school?" I asked.

"Okay," he said.

"What grade are you in now?" I asked.

His face had begun to return to its usual shade of dead-fish-belly white, but with my questions the color came back in a rush. "Junior," he said.

"One more year!" I said, smiling brightly.

"Yeah, right," he said. "I read one of your books," he added; these being the most words I'd ever heard Brad McLemore mutter in succession.

It was my turn to blush. I write romance novels— of the bodice-ripping variety. "You did?" I said lamely, trying to find something to look at other than him.

"Yeah. My mother had it. I dug it out of the trash when she was through with it."

I opted not to get pissy about his mother's choice of book depositories, and said, "Well. What did you think?"

"Interesting," he opined.

I heard the stampede on the stairs and in a flash both girls were back in the kitchen, grabbing on to a hip of mine each, followed shortly by Conner, Brad's younger brother and my son Graham's best friend. The eight-year-old version of Eddie Haskell, and the most polite boy you'll meet outside of a sitcom.

Conner was everything his older brother was not. Blond hair neatly trimmed, he wore pressed and creased khakis, a buttoned-down Oxford cloth shirt, and his smile was a dentist's dream. And it was aimed my way with a vengeance.

"Thank you so much for having me over, Mrs. Pugh," Eddie—I mean Conner—said. "It's always a pleasure being in your lovely home."

"Thank you, Conner," I said, walking them both to the back door. "Come back any time."

"Thank you so much," Conner said, smiling brightly. He waved and was out the door behind his brother. As they rounded the corner, I heard Brad demand that Conner hurry up. Conner's reply: "Shut your mouth, pizza face."

I made my way back to the laundry room while dragging the girls, and I had just started my next-to-the-last load when the phone rang. I managed to get out and over to the new portable without a clinging growth in the shape of a girl child and answered the phone.

"Hello?"

"Is this 555-7525?" a voice asked.

"Who's calling?" I asked.

"This is Codderville Emergency 911, ma'am. Are you having a problem?"

I wondered fleetingly if things were so dull in our little town that the 911 operators were having to drum up business. "No, no problem. What's going on?"

"Do you have small children, ma'am?" a female operator asked.

Some trouble the year before had left me with what I like to think of as healthy paranoia. Which means always answer a question with a question. "Would you please tell me why you're calling?"

"We just got a call from this number, ma'am, but the party hung up."

"Well, we didn't call."

"If you have small children, Mrs. Pugh—"

"How do you know my name?" I demanded.

"The electronic readout, ma'am. The call comes in, we know immediately what number it's coming from, the address, and who lives there. You are Mrs. Pugh?"

"Yes, I am. Hold on just a minute."

I put my hand over the mouth piece of the phone and yelled for my son Graham. He came to the head of the stairs and glared down at me.

"What?" he demanded.

"Did you call 911 and hang up?"

He rolled his eyes and turned around.

"Graham!" I yelled. "Answer me."

He turned his head only slightly. "No, I did not."

"You better not be lying to me."

The eyes rolled again and he turned to face me fully. "Mother, I only lie to you when it's important."

"This is important!" I said.

"Not to me," Graham said, heading for his room.

I got back on the phone with the 911 operator. "I just asked my children and they said they hadn't been playing with the phone. Besides," I lied, "my children wouldn't do anything like that." Then it hit me. "But we just got this new cordless phone and we've been having some trouble with it—getting neighbors' phone calls, stuff like that. Could it be some electronic problem?"

"That's a possibility," the operator said grudgingly. "But if I were you, I'd get some locks for the phones to insure that your children don't make crank calls."

"My children don't do things like—"

The line disconnected.

The wonderful thing about each of my girls turning five is that they are now in kindergarten. Megan turned five in May of last year, Bessie in August, which made them both eligible to go to the public school. Not only did this save us a bundle at the Montessori, the public school in Black Cat Ridge has an after-school program that keeps kindergartners (who usually attend from eight until noon) as long as you want them kept. (Well, that's an exaggeration. When I suggested I'd come back in the fall to pick them up, the caregiver glared at me, which just goes to show how erroneous some advertising can be.) But it does allow me to leave them at the school until Graham, my fourth-grader, gets out at three. That way, instead of the measly four hours I used to have to myself, I now have seven blessed hours all to my lonesome. And believe me, lonesome I'm not. I read about women with the "empty nest syndrome" and wonder if they also like to shove sharp needles into their eyeballs.

You're right, I'm not likely to win the mother of the year award from anybody. You see, I never planned on having children. I was never one of those little girls who played with dolls and wanted twenty-seven children all named Tammy-something. I really hadn't made the decision *not* to have children until my senior year in college. At that time I'd worked very hard for a degree in English with a minor in elementary education. My senior year was when I did my student teaching. I lasted thirty-two minutes before I ran screaming from Highland Park Elementary School with the idea full blown and set in stone in my mind that the closest I ever wanted to get to a child again was on the other side of the cage bars.

Now I have three children: two accidents and Bessie, the child we inherited. Not that I don't love them, I do. It's strange how much I love them. But hey, I need a life too, you know.

So I was in my office working on my latest bodice-ripping saga when the second erroneous 911 call came. It was 1:30 in the afternoon and my children were at school. It was the same thing, different operator. Which meant explaining all over again about the cordless phone and the electronic problems. The male operator also asked if I had small children at home. I told him they were at school and couldn't have done it even if they were the type, which they weren't. A mother has to have some pride in her offspring. Even false pride.

It was almost exactly a week after the first 911 phone call when I went into town to have lunch with my husband. I don't do that often, because when he has work he's usually very busy, and when he doesn't have work he's too depressed to be a fun lunch date. But I'd had to go into Codderville for computer paper at the store one building over from Willis's. It seemed dumb not to try.

It was March in central Texas, which means I'd bundled the kids up in winter clothes that morning and now felt guilty because they were probably all dying of heat prostration since the temperature had climbed to seventy-five degrees and the sun was brilliant. Of course, being March in central Texas, there was always the possibility that by the time they got out at three o'clock it could be thirty-two degrees and sleeting. It's been known to happen, and this is no exaggeration. I drove the five miles from Black Cat Ridge to Codderville, crossing the Colorado River, with the window down on the driver's side of the station wagon, pretending I was in a Porsche convertible traversing the autobahn with a guy named Sven at my side, and eventually pulled into the parking lot of Willis's building.

Willis's former secretary, Rosie Morales, had finally left the firm to attend school full time in Houston, and now he had a new young woman working the outer office. Rosie and I had been pretty close, and I, of course, slightly resented the new girl, Angel Wasserman. But not all that much. She wasn't as pretty as Rosie; she was five-two, painfully thin with a horsey face covered with entirely too much inexpertly applied makeup, hair several shades of bottled blond, in such bad condition it actually screamed for a hot oil treatment. She wasn't much of a threat to my marriage. Not that Willis is the type to look at another woman. *Ha.* Truthfully, he has full permission to look—but that's all—and I've always felt pretty secure about his fidelity.

Angel was the only one in the outer office when I walked in, and she was busily banging away at the word processor. She turned and smiled and said, "May I help you?" in her wispy, little girl voice, obviously forgetting who I was and what an exalted position I held.

I smiled. "Hi, I'm E.J. Willis's wife?"

"Oh," she said, playfully slapping herself on the forehead. "Jeez, I'm sorry. My brain's atrophied from staring at this stupid computer screen. Hi, Miz Pugh. Let me tell Willis you're here."

She jumped up and stuck her head in the door of the big room (the office suite consisted of the reception room, Willis's private office, and the big room, which held the drafting boards, conference table, coffee machine, computers with AutoCAD systems, and supply cabinets. Willis could usually be found in there rather than his private office) and told Willis I was there.

He came out a second later grinning from ear to ear. Which is always a nice way for a husband of twelve years to look at his wife. And it was also one of his nicest looks. He's got a world-class smile, my husband does, and he is fully aware of it. Six-foot-two, two hundred and forty generally firm pounds, blond hair and dark brown eyes, and a killer smile. And all mine. And at five feet eleven inches (and with what some would graciously call a Rubenesque figure), he fit me well.

"Got time for a quick lunch?" I asked, grinning back at him.

He walked up and kissed me on the cheek. "Unfortunately the Motel 6 is closed," he said.

"Damn, I guess we'll just have to eat."

"Where?"

"What have you got cash for?" I asked.

"You ask me to lunch and I have to pay?"

"And be happy about it."

He pulled his wallet out and peered in. "McDonald's?"

"Fine," I said, heading for the door.

"Can we bring you anything back, Angel?" my husband asked his new secretary. (Which is only proper: at least he didn't invite her along.)

"Big Mac and fries?" she said, reaching for her purse.

Willis waved her money away. "On me," he said and we were out the door.

"Oh," I asked as we got on the elevator, "did you get that info for me?"

Willis is into esoteric and antique firearms (he doesn't buy them, we can't afford it, but he likes to find out things about them), and he does research for me when I have a scene in a book that calls for his expertise.

"Yeah, I found some on the Info-Net that looks like what you need. I'll have Angel send it over on the modem. Just call her when you get back home."

We met Doug Kingsley coming in the front door of the building. Doug was an engineering consultant who'd been working with Willis on his new project, with a possibility of becoming a full partner. Willis and I had stayed up late many a night discussing the pros and cons of taking Doug on as a partner.

Willis is an electrical engineer and had worked most of our lives since college for various oil-related companies in Houston. Four years ago we made the big move, with Willis opening his own engineering consulting firm and moving the family from Houston to Willis's hometown of Codderville. I, needless to say, wasn't thrilled about moving to the same town as his mother, but Black Cat Ridge was in its earliest stages of development then—a totally separated full-service community on the *other* side of the Colorado River from Codderville, so I agreed hoping for lots of hell and high water to keep my mother-in-law away.

Things have been tight financially since the move, and thus there was both a pro and a con of taking Doug on as a partner: pro: he could help generate more revenue; con: he'd be taking half of our income.

Another of the pros, however, for me, anyway, was that Doug was more than comfortable on the eyes. About my height, he was slender, with dark hair and blue eyes and a finely chiseled face that led some women (this one included) to think in terms of Hollywood and the silver screen. He was gorgeous and nice. A strange combination, but it can happen.

He grinned when he saw us. "Where you two headed?" he asked.

"McDonald's," I answered. "Want to come?" Hav-

ing Angel join us for lunch was one thing, but having
Doug Kingsley along was quite another.

He did a quick about-face. "Best offer I've had this
week," he said, holding the door open for me.

We took my car to the McDonald's about a mile
up the highway and sat and talked amid somebody
else's squalling kids. It's amazing how I don't hear
other people's children screaming anymore. If it's not
mine, I don't care. Like water off a duck's back.

The lunchtime conversation went the way of electronics, which all conversations do when you are sitting with two or more engineers. To keep myself in
the conversation, I told them both about the 911 calls
and asked about the possibility of electronic
malfunction.

"Honey, why didn't you tell me about this?" Willis asked.

I shrugged. "Forgot. With everything that goes on
in my day, Willis, you're lucky I occasionally fix
dinner."

My husband's eyes got big. "Oh, you're going to
start doing that?"

I took a whack at him and Doug laughed. "Now,
if you two could guarantee me marriage is always
like what you have, I might try it."

"No marriage is like what we have," Willis said.
"If it was, the institution would have died off long
ago."

"That's not true," I said, kicking my husband's leg
under the table. Why are men always trying to talk
other men out of marriage? Of course, women prefer
all men to be married so their husbands have no
other lifestyles with which to compare their own. Or
at least that's one theory. "We have a perfectly normal relationship. All a good marriage needs is total
devotion and fidelity."

"Well, forget that," Doug said, laughing. "Now,
about your electronics problem. There could be a

problem with another cordless phone in your neighborhood. Especially if it's the same brand. Do you have 911 on speed dial?"

"No," I said.

"Yeah," Willis said, leaning toward Doug, "if it was on speed dial and another phone in the neighborhood on the same system punched the same number, it could cross. Possibly."

"But I haven't put in any speed dial numbers on this phone," I said. But they weren't paying attention. They were deep into a discussion of the components of cordless phones that could allow this possibility, and the variations of other possibilities. I stopped listening and ate my Big Mac.

As we left, we got Angel's Big Mac and fries and I dropped off the two men at the Oak Hills Office Tower, which had formerly been a nice little hill covered with nice little oaks. The developers, in what passes for developer-wisdom, graded the hill and removed all those nasty trees to make room for the office building; now, the only thing left to remind its occupants of the oaks and the hill was merely the name.

When I got home I barely had time to call up Angel and have her send Willis's information over on the modem before I had to take off and pick up the kids. My day does not allow for work, a leisurely lunch, *and* the responsibilities of motherhood.

The afterschool day-care is held in the small school gym, and Graham usually picks up the girls there. The three of them then come out to meet me where I'm usually already parked in a long line of other parents (okay, mothers) there to do the exact same thing. I saw Graham coming out of the building with Megan in tow, and my heart did a flip-flop on not seeing Bessie. Only seconds later, however, the door Graham had let slam shut behind him opened and

Miss Martha, Bessie's kindergarten teacher, came out holding Bessie's hand.

It didn't take a rocket scientist to know that there was a problem. Miss Martha, a gorgeous but humorless lady in her mid-thirties with Dolly Parton hair and bosom, didn't hang around after her class was out unless there was a problem with a capital P.

I pulled the car out of line and found a parking spot marked PRINCIPAL and stopped the car, getting out and weaving my way through the standing cars to meet my children and Miss Martha.

"Hi, Miss Martha," I said brightly.

She didn't return my cheery manner nor my gracious smile. "Mrs. Pugh, could we speak a moment, please?"

"Certainly," I said, showing off the results of my teenaged orthodontics to its fullest. "Graham, sweetheart, could you walk your sisters to the car, please?"

He rolled his eyes, either at the "sweetheart," the "please," or the general uppitiness of the request itself, but complied, while I watched the three of them wend their way through the now-moving carloads of mothers and offspring. When they got to the car, I turned to Miss Martha.

"How can I help you?" I asked, hoping against hope she needed a volunteer for a field trip (which I could politely decline) or a couple dozen cookies (which I could pick up cheap at the supermarket). No such luck.

"We have a problem, Mrs. Pugh," Miss Martha said, crossing her hands primly in front of her three hundred dollar sweater, diamonds winking on her fingers. (I've figured out that, at least in the more affluent suburbs, it takes an independently wealthy woman or one married to a fairly well-off man to be able to afford to teach school.)

"Oh?" I said, dropping the perfect smile and replacing it with a concerned-parent frown.

"It's Bessie."

Well, since she was the one in Miss Martha's class, I didn't think it concerned one of the others.

"And?" I said, moving my head slightly to one side, the I'm-still-concerned-but-you're-beginning-to-annoy-me stance.

"Children are very impressionable, Mrs. Pugh." It was a declarative statement. I accepted it as such.

Nodding my head in encouragement, I said, "That's true."

"They're aware of every little thing we say and do."

I turned and looked pointedly at my station wagon. It was bouncing up and down in my children's attempt to destroy it. They would, I knew, succeed in something under fifteen minutes. "Your point is?" I said, my way of encouraging her.

"It's Bessie's language, Mrs. Pugh."

Bessie? Language? With the other two—my flesh and blood—anything was possible. But Bessie came from a decidedly more refined gene pool.

"Just what exactly did she say, Miss Martha?"

"She used the *f*-word and the *sh*-word."

I started to ask if she'd used them correctly in a sentence, but decided that probably wasn't a good idea. Instead, I just looked shocked and said, "Bessie?"

"And," Miss Martha went on, her voice getting lower, with just a slight edge to it, "when I asked her where she heard such language, she said, and I quote, Mrs. Pugh, 'at home'."

Thinking quickly, I said, "We have cable."

This, apparently, didn't daunt Miss Martha. "Little pitchers have big ears, Mrs. Pugh. We have a responsibility to our children to teach them the wonders of the world, not to wallow in filth."

I always wondered about little pitchers and big ears. Actually, pitchers have spouts and handles.

They don't have ears at all. I nodded my head. "I'll have a talk with Bessie. Thank you for coming to me with this."

"I think we serve our children best by example, Mrs. Pugh."

"So true," I said, smiling. "Thank you again." I headed for the car before my children could manage to disassemble the engine.

The third 911 call came a few minutes before midnight that night. Willis caught the phone before I did, which is always a problem because he can have a conversation for several minutes before he's fully awake. He finally turned toward me and accused, "Did you call 911?"

I rolled my eyes. "I told you about that today!"

"Oh," he said and got back on the phone to explain the situation to, I'm sure, a totally different 911 operator.

I slipped out of bed and went to the door of Graham's room. Opening it, I peeked in, only to find him sound asleep. The nearest phone to him would have been downstairs or the one in our bedroom. I don't believe in children having phones in their rooms. I figured I'd save that privilege for when they're surly teenagers and I'd just as soon not have them around.

I crawled back into bed. Willis leaned over and said, "That prick."

"What prick?" I asked.

"The 911 operator. He said to put locks on the phones so our kids wouldn't make crank calls. I said our kids don't make crank calls."

I nodded my head. "Yeah, I checked. Graham's sound asleep."

"The operator said by their records this is the third erroneous 911 call we've made."

I sat up. "But we didn't make the damned calls!"

"I know that! I told him that. Shit." Willis rolled over. "Let's try to get some sleep. I have a big day tomorrow."

Like I didn't. I rolled over and thought nasty thoughts about the 911 service in Codderville. Tomorrow, I decided, I'm going to call the supervisor down there and get this straightened out.

Naturally, I forgot to do that. It would have been preferable if I had.

Friday afternoons my children are a little more outrageous than on an average weekday. It probably has to do with the coming weekend, thoughts of freedom from school, that kind of thing. When something bad happens, it's usually on a Friday. Like the time Graham got caught breaking windows in an empty house two blocks over; or the time I caught Megan and Bessie putting Bert and Ernie in the dryer; or the time Megan and Bessie convinced the four-year-old boy across the street to show them his pee-pee. All on a Friday.

This Friday was no exception. Graham had left his schoolbag on the playground. He didn't tell me this until we'd pulled in the driveway at home, which necessitated driving all the way back to the school to find it. Megan had her nose out of joint about some girl named Melissa who had said something at school that Bessie had laughed at. Bessie refused to tell Megan what Melissa had said. In her rush to get out of the car and away from her sister, Bessie slipped and skinned her knee on the driveway, which resulted in a lot of tears, recriminations, and iodine.

The only saving grace of that particular Friday was that the sun was out and the backyard was relatively dry. I shooed them and all the cats outside after their afternoon snacks and sat down to watch *Oprah*. I'd barely sorted out the panel and who was sleeping with whom when. Graham burst in through the back door.

"Mom! I told her not to! Mom! I told her!"

I jumped up and ran to the back door. "What is it?"

"There was a Hershey's Kiss sitting on the picnic table and Megan ate it and I told her not to—"

Megan was kneeling on the cobblestone patio. Blood was pouring from her mouth.

"Oh, my God!" I knelt beside her. "Did you swallow any?"

She shook her head, her eyes huge.

"Spit!" I said. "Spit it all out!" I turned to my son. "Graham, call 911!" I shouted, trying to be heard over Bessie's screams. Bessie has a problem with blood. A problem that started when her birth family was murdered in her presence.

Graham ran into the house while I held my daughter and tried to see if all the glass and chocolate were out of her mouth. In less than a minute Graham had returned with the portable phone in his hand and the first tears I'd seen in his eyes since he broke his toe at age three.

"Mama," he said, "they told me to stop playing with the phone. They won't come."

Two

I grabbed the portable phone from Graham's hand and called 911 myself. It took two precious minutes to convince them there was a real emergency. Once I knew they were on their way, I knelt beside Megan, gingerly trying to check her mouth for glass. There was so much blood, and my hands were shaking so much, it was hard to see. I'm not sure when Bessie's screams stopped, but when I noticed the silence I looked up to place her. Graham had her on the swing set, sitting in a swing, his arms around her, his mouth near her ear. She had her eyes closed, as if she were listening intently to what he said. At that moment I wanted to give him a medal, a citation for thinking on his feet, and a great big hug. He might have accepted the medal. There was a Codderville emergency unit at the door in about four minutes, although it seemed to take a lifetime.

Brad McLemore sauntered into the backyard about

the same time as the paramedics, looking for Conner. He stood there for a minute with a stupid expression on his face while the paramedics bent over my daughter.

When one of the paramedics said they would have to take Megan to the hospital, I grabbed Brad by the arm.

"I need to go with her in the ambulance. Can you stay with Bessie and Graham?"

"Huh? Yeah, okay," he said, shrugging skinny shoulders.

"Graham!" I called.

Graham led Bessie by the hand to the gate where I was standing, ready to rush to the ambulance. "Brad's going to stay with you until Daddy gets here. Call Daddy and tell him what happened and have him come home right away, okay, honey?"

"Okay, sure, whatever," Graham the gallant said.

That was the plan, except Willis came to the hospital instead, leaving Graham and Bessie in the care of Brad McLemore longer than I would have liked. But I couldn't blame Willis: I wouldn't have wanted to be the one at home awaiting word of our daughter's fate.

The waiting room was full to capacity with car-wreck victims, a stabbing, a lady who'd sliced off her thumb while cutting up a chicken, and an assortment of children with everything from whooping cough to beans up their noses. Willis and I had sat vigil silently, holding hands, unable to fathom what would happen if some of that glass had gotten into Megan's system, what vital organs could be in jeopardy.

They finally let us back in to be with her. The emergency room doctor had felt for slivers of glass, flushed her stomach, used a magnifier and an endoscope to search for glass in her mouth and stomach. Megan had said she hadn't swallowed the candy and she'd been right. There were several tiny cuts in her mouth and one larger one, but even that didn't need stitches. She had to rinse her mouth out with Listerine five times a day and keep on a liquid diet until Monday, when we would at last see our family doctor.

Willis dropped Megan and me off at the house and went to grab some fried chicken to go. It was almost seven and dinner wasn't exactly on my mind. The downstairs was quiet when I walked in the front door. I was opening my mouth to holler for someone when Brad walked down the stairs.

"She okay?" he said, pointing at Megan.

"She'll be fine," I said, smiling at my daughter. "Some cuts but no glass and that's what matters."

"Uh-huh," Brad said.

"Where are the kids?" I asked.

Brad pointed up the stairs. "Their rooms," he said.

I opened my purse and pulled out a handful of bills. "Look, Brad, I really appreciate you helping us out. I had no idea it would take this long—"

He took the bills out of my hand, said, "No sweat," and walked out the front door.

I took Megan upstairs. Bessie was in the room she shared with Megan, and she was glad to see her sister alive and well. Graham was in his room, reading a trashy comic book.

It wasn't until later that night that I'd noticed things in my jewelry box messed up, rearranged. I don't have a lot of good jewelry, mainly because Willis and I were married in the seventies and when he proposed and asked if I wanted a ring, I'd stupidly said, "Who needs material things like jewelry? All I need is your love." Which, for some reason, seemed to give him carte blanche to buy me little more than naughty underwear as significant gifts most of our married life. But I did have a few good pieces mixed in with the costume jewelry. Nothing was missing, but someone had obviously gone through it.

My first thought was of Brad, although I tried to dismiss it, considering the fact that I have three children, two of them girls who like to play dress-up and have been known to go through my things uninvited. But there was something about the kid next door that sent a chill up my spine.

Have you ever tried to rinse a five-year-old's mouth out with Listerine? Even once, much less five times a day? I was lucky it happened on the weekend so that I had Willis there to hold her while I poured the stuff into her mouth. Even then, there was more Listerine on my clothes than in her mouth.

I called Elena Luna, the detective at the Codderville Sheriff's Office who I'd gotten to know fairly well the year before, and told her about the glass-laced Hershey's Kiss.

"Is Megan okay?" was her first question, being the mother of two sons herself.

"None of it went any farther than her mouth. She's got some cuts, but she'll be okay."

"Thank God. Where did the candy come from?"

"I have no earthly idea. It was just there, Graham said, sitting on the picnic table."

"Who has access to your backyard?" Luna asked.

"Anybody who has the wherewithal to pull the latch, Luna. I mean, we're not exactly Fort Knox with security around here."

"I've noticed." I could hear her sigh on the other end of the line. "Look, I'll call around, see if this has happened with anybody else. Have somebody call the schools and warn the kids to stay away from unknown sources of goodies. Which they should already know," she said, an edge to her voice.

"You think I didn't tell Megan that a million times?

A trillion times? You know kids!" I was almost shouting my guilt across the miles.

Luna sighed again. "I know. Believe me, I know. It's the things you don't tell them that really get to you. Like who would have thought to mention to a two-year-old not to climb up to the top bunk and throw a baseball bat down on his brother's head?"

"Luis?" I asked, picturing her youngest son, now twelve.

"Eduardo had a lump the size of a softball for about a week." We both laughed. "Look," she said, "I'm really sorry about Megan. I'll do what I can about finding out where it could have come from, but don't hold your breath."

"I rarely do," I said. "I tend to pass out after a few hours."

On Saturday, Willis went around to all the neighbors with small children and warned them about the nasty treat, asking if they'd heard of any similar incidents. None had.

It was that afternoon that Miss Martha's warning came back to haunt me. The girls were sitting in the living room playing with Barbies. Megan attempted to say something to Bessie, but because of the damage to her mouth, it came out garbled. Sweet little Bessie said, "Shit, you talk funny!" and giggled up a storm.

Willis was in the garage. I marched out there and declared, "We have to stop cussing."

He turned from his manly chore (something to do with tools) and looked at me. "I don't do dope, I don't smoke, I rarely drink, and I don't mess around on you. Why are you attempting to rip away my only remaining vice?"

I gave him a blow-by-blow of my discussion with Miss Martha. Willis groaned. "You're right. It's one thing to corrupt Megan and Graham, but Bessie . . ."

I nodded my head in shame.

"Okay," he said.

And I knew that was going to be that. In college and while we lived in Mexico, Willis smoked marijuana, did coke on the weekends, and an occasional hallucinogen. I only smoked a very occasional joint. When we decided to move back to the states, Willis said, "Well, enough dope. They're serious about it up there." And stopped. Cold turkey. I went into marijuana withdrawal and ended up gaining ten pounds.

When I was pregnant with Graham, Willis decided to give up a three-pack-a-day cigarette habit. I smoked less than half a pack a day, but knew it was even more important that I quit. He quit cold turkey. I got hypnotized, behavior modified, and gained thirty pounds. Only about fifteen of it baby-related.

So I knew now that Willis would quit cussing. Just like that. I went back in the house and raided the refrigerator.

Sunday the kids and I set up a cussing jar—an empty, clean mayonnaise jar with a slit in the lid into which quarters would be dropped for every cuss word uttered by a member of the family. I gave the kids a dollar's worth of quarters each, telling them they could spend them however they wanted and wouldn't that be better than cussing? Graham immediately said "shit" four times and dropped all of his in the jar, grinned, and walked outside to play.

Monday morning I took Megan to our family doctor. She got a clean bill of health from the doctor, who said she could start eating solids and we could lessen the Listerine rinses down to one a day, at bedtime after she brushed her teeth. I dropped her off at school and went straight to Willis's office to pick him up for our interview with Mr. Colburn, the bureaucrat from hell.

Although it was fifty degrees out, there was a piercing wind from the north, the kind that led Texans to coin such time-honored phrases as "nothing 'tween us and Canada but a barbed wire fence." I was cold, my fingers were numb, the heater in the station wagon didn't work, and I had a hole in the toe of one sneaker that let in an amazing amount of frigid air. That was just enough to get me in the right mood to deal with the director of the Codder County Emergency Services.

"I cannot believe you allowed this to happen! This is insane!"

"Mrs. Pugh, you're spitting on my desk," he said.

"E.J." Willis grabbed my arm and lowered me back into my chair.

"My child was bleeding! My son called 911—just like we taught him to do! Just like the Codderville ISD taught him to do—" I was standing again. Willis grabbed the waist of my jeans and pulled me back into the chair.

"Mrs. Pugh, my operators have had several errone-ous calls from your address—"

"Each one of which we explained to your people!" I shouted. "It was electronic! I told them that!"

"If you had come to me and explained the situa-tion instead of telling each of the separate opera-tors—Mrs. Pugh, we have fourteen operators over a twenty-four hour, seven-day-a-week span. They can't be expected to all know that you were having elec-tronic problems—"

"Why not?" I shouted, unable to jump up due to the restraining hand on my waistband. "They all cer-tainly knew about the calls, right? That's why they refused us service when we had a real emergency, right? If they knew about the calls, why wasn't there a flag telling them we weren't responsible for those calls? Huh?"

"Because we've never established that to be a fact, Mrs. Pugh," Mr. Colburn said. Because he was a city employee, his face was red in his obvious attempt to keep from telling off a taxpayer—his boss, if you will.

"Mr. Colburn," Willis said, the model of decorum, "I hope you can understand our concern. Our little girl was injured. You understand the problems that would have ensued if your people had not finally responded or if their delay had caused our daughter damage?"

Oh, goody, I thought, he's talking litigation. That should put the fear of God into the pompous ass.

"I just say that all's well that ends well," Mr. Colburn said.

"Like hell!" I shouted. Willis had let go of my jeans and I sprang up so fast I almost landed on top of Mr. Colburn's desk. "All is not well, Mr. Colburn. I am not happy and things are never well when I am not happy, Mr. Colburn. Just ask my husband!"

Willis stood up next to me. "Mr. Colburn, have we any guarantee this won't happen again?"

Mr. Colburn also stood. "I can assure you, Mr. Pugh, that we will try to rectify this situation. As for your, excuse me, electronic problems—"

"Yes?" I said icily.

He smiled. "I would suggest you take that up with the manufacturer of your cordless phone. We are not responsible for malfunctioning electronic equipment in your home, Mrs. Pugh."

Willis pulled me out of the office while I was still thinking of a scathing comeback that would have put Mr. Colburn forever in his place. I hate it when Willis does that.

I drove home, leaving Codderville behind as I crossed the Colorado River and headed into Black Cat Ridge. Black Cat Ridge is a very large subdivision, almost a town unto itself, with stores and a fire station auxiliary. We have our own elementary and middle schools, but we're under the umbrella of the

Codderville School District. Codderville is an old town, built during the oil boom. Black Cat Ridge is new, less than five years old, and a lot of its residents are commuters to Austin, an hour and a half to the west, and even some to Houston, over two hours to the east.

As I pulled onto Sage Brush Trail, our street, I passed the house on the corner. As I always do. It had been the Lesters' house, Bessie's birth family. Roy and Terry Lester had been our best friends. Their son Aldon, though three years older than Graham, had been his best friend, his idol. Their daughter Monique had been our baby-sitter. They'd all been murdered a little less than a year ago. In finding out what had happened to them, our home had been set ablaze and, as executors of Roy and Terry's estate, and guardian of Bessie, we'd moved into the house next door for six months while we went through endless insurance and remodeling hassles.

Six months ago we'd moved back into our own home and put the Lester house on the market. It had sold quickly, even though we never tried to hide its history. The McLemores bought it and with it came Graham's new best friend, Conner.

Every three years Terry and I had watched as Willis helped Roy paint the trim of the white brick house periwinkle blue. Now the trim was white. Terry and I had laughed every spring when Roy, with Willis's help, had tried to trim the bushes in front of the house into a topiary, though never quite achieving his goal of rabbit, bird, or whatever. Now the bushes were gone.

I hadn't stepped foot inside the Lester house since the day the McLemores moved in. I'd invited Ginger, Mrs. McLemore, over for coffee on several occasions, but she always, graciously, had something else to do. I could tell on the day they moved in that Ginger McLemore and I were not the same sort. On moving day she was wearing a coordinated jogging suit, every blond hair perfection, and her nails were done. Since that day I'd yet to see her mussed. The woman obviously never endured PMS, never had a bad hair day, and the only reason she wasn't doing toothpaste commercials was because she didn't live in LA.

The only person in my family who'd been in the house next door since the McLemores had moved in was Graham, and try as I might to drill him, an eight-year-old boy just doesn't know the difference between French provincial and English Tudor, Country French and Early American. I'd had to be happy with the fact that he was pretty sure there was a couch in the living room and he thought it might be sorta white.

Our relationship with Arthur McLemore, husband and father, wasn't much better. Two to four years older than his wife and three to five inches taller, Arthur was Ginger's perfect mate. But, of course, any woman who could maintain a tan like Ginger's would know exactly which man to pick.

Arthur was a jovial sort, of the boorish variety, and liked to corner anyone who walked out of their house while he was outside. Willis, during his semimonthly run, had started going out of his way to avoid the McLemore house from fear of having to endure an endless monologue on Arthur McLemore's golf handicap.

I found myself studying the McLemore house as I pulled into my driveway, which was adjacent to theirs. Conner McLemore was a smarmy, manipulating little brat. He was fairly easy to get a handle on. Brad McLemore was an altogether different story. It would have been easy to just mark him off as a typical, nasty, surly teenaged boy—too easy. I thought again about the hands that may or may not have been rummaging through my jewelry box. I decided Brad McLemore would definitely not be filling the baby-sitting vacancy left by my friend Monique, and he wouldn't be left alone again in my home for any reason short of an emergency.

I went inside and cleaned up the breakfast dishes, put some chicken out to defrost for dinner, and moved into my cubbyhole of an office to work on my latest project, *Reflections in Turquoise*, which I hadn't touched since the Friday of Megan's accident. I was just getting to the good part. I'd gone through one hundred and fourteen pages of foreplay between my heroine and my hero. He was Branson Calhoun, head cowboy on the ranch now owned by my heroine, easterner Lavana Merchant, the virgin widow of Marcel Merchant, and now we were getting down to the dirty deed. I booted up, hit the key that would bring me the newest chapter, and found the entire scene already written.

One of the rules of romance writing is that we can put in all the sex we want, but because these books are written for women, the sex is implied, using lots of arousal words, never graphic. The words on the screen were not words I would have written—any time—any place. It was a vile, pornographic, violent, explicit scene. It made my skin crawl as I read it.

Leaving the screen up, I left the room and went into the kitchen to call Willis.

When he finally got on the phone, I asked, "Have you been messing with my computer?"

"No, why?"

"Can you come home for a minute?"

"Baby, I'm right in the middle of some—"

"Now, Willis. Please."

I hung up and went back to my cubbyhole, standing in the doorway and staring at the screen of my computer. Willis got there about fifteen minutes later. Coming in the back door, he could see me standing at the doorway of the closet under the stairs that served as my office.

"Jeez, Eej, this better be important. I have about a million things to do on this project."

"Come here." He came. I pointed at the screen. "Sit down and read that."

He did. After a minute or two, he looked up. "You didn't write this," he said.

"No," I said. "I didn't."

"Jesus H. Christ." He scrolled back to the beginning of the scene and read it again. "My God. How did this get on here?"

"That's what I'd like to know."

"Well, I'm erasing it—"

"No!" I grabbed his arm. "Let's make a copy of it first. Just in case."

Willis gave me one of his looks. "Getting a little paranoid, are we?"

I pushed him out of the chair and sat down to print out the filth. "Getting a lot paranoid," I said. "Under the circumstances."

He stood over me, watching me print out. "What circumstances?"

"These 911 calls. The glass-laced Hershey's Kiss. Someone going through my jewelry box—"

"What?" He swiveled my chair around to face him. "What's this about your jewelry box?"

So I told him. And told him about my suspicions of Brad McLemore. "Well, yeah," Willis said, "he's strange. But not any stranger than most teenagers—"

"This from someone who once professed to the belief of never trusting anyone over thirty?"

"Yeah, well, that was before I turned thirty, okay? Anyway, you think he did this while he was in the house? While we had Megan at the hospital?"

"He told me last week that he'd read one of my books. Seems like a natural progression."

"From reading one to writing one?"

"I don't know!" I said, jumping up from my chair in exasperation and going into the kitchen. "I don't know what's going on, but I don't feel really comfortable with any of this."

He put his arms around me and nuzzled my neck. "I don't know what's going on either, babe, but let's not let it get to us, okay? I've gotta get back to work. You gonna be okay?"

I sighed. "Yes, I'll be fine. Go."

After he left I took the printed-out porn pages and put them in a manila envelope, hiding the envelope deep in one of my filing drawers, and erased the garbage from the computer screen, then turned the whole thing off. I had a deadline, but after reading the filth that had been on the screen, I had no desire for Lavana and Branson to do the dirty deed. Washing clothes was preferable.

My house and the house next door both have detached garages. The garages sit side by side, with two double-wide driveways running up to them. There'd never been any separation between the driveways when the Lesters had lived there. Now for some unknown reason there was a foot-high white picket fence (which certainly didn't keep the kids from stepping over it) separating the two driveways. When I left my house to go pick up the kids from school, Brad McLemore was shooting hoops in his driveway.

"You're out of school early," I said, walking around to the driver's side of the car.

"Yeah."

I got in and backed out. When I turned my head back around as I pulled onto the street, Brad McLemore was standing in the driveway, holding the basketball, and staring at my departing car.

I drove to the school, trying not to think of the boy next door. I got the kids piled into the station wagon and headed for home, stopping only briefly for a gallon of milk at the corner store. When I got back, the City of Codderville was well-represented in my driveway by two fire trucks, a police car, and an ambulance. And a fireman was busily hacking away at my front door with an ax.

Three

"Uh, Mom," Graham said, pointing at the front of our house where all the unusual activity seemed to be concentrated. I looked at my children. All three were wide-eyed in wonderment.

I pulled the car over to the curb across the street from our house and shut off the engine. Turning to Graham I said, "Stay in the car. Keep your sisters in the car. Nobody moves. Do you understand?"

"Yeah, right," he said, eyes glued to our front door, the wood of which we could hear splintering from where we were.

"Oh, God," I said and jumped out of the car and ran across the street. "Excuse me," I said to a heavy-jacketed fireman. "Excuse me."

He turned my direction. "Lady, get back. We're working here."

"I realize that, but this is my house you're working on."

31

He finally looked at me. "Yeah?" he said.

"Yeah. May I ask why you're breaking down my door?" I held up the key to the front door to show him an alternative means of entry.

"We got a 911 call saying the house was on fire and somebody was trapped in a bedroom upstairs."

"I don't see any smoke! Besides, there shouldn't be anybody in my house—"

The sound of wood breaking through halted my words. I looked at my house. My front door lay in splintered ruins across the threshold as firemen bounced on it running into my home, fully suited and wearing gas masks. No smoke billowed out from the open door. One cat, however, did peek a head out, then withdrew rapidly at the onslaught of more human animals.

The crux of the upheaval was that there was no one in my house. There was no fire or smoke in my house. Not even one of the cats stuck in a tree. After the City of Codderville emergency personnel (all fifteen of them) had departed, I called Willis.

"We no longer have a front door," I said, once he was on the line.

"Why not?" he asked, reasonably for him.

So I told him. An hour later Willis had finished nailing the sheet of plywood to the front of the house that he'd brought back with him from Codderville.

"We're supposed to sleep with only a piece of plywood between the world and us?"

"Like oak was a great deterrent to an ax," he said.

I gave him a look. "I'll buy a metal door at the hardware store tomorrow. Maybe Doug will help me hang it. Meanwhile," he said, as we walked around the house to the back door (we'd boarded ourselves out of our home), "let's go have a talk with Mr. Colburn."

"This is the silliest, stupidest—"

"Have you thought about seeing a dentist, Mrs. Pugh? You're spitting on my desk again."

"Colburn, look," Willis said. "We don't have a front door. We have three frightened children. My wife is close to the breaking point—"

"Or the point of breaking something!" I said, ominously looking at Mr. Colburn's neck.

Mr. Colburn stood and leaned on his desk, glaring at us. "First you're upset because we didn't respond quickly enough to one of your calls, now you're upset because we responded at all! Give me a break!"

"We didn't call!" Willis and I yelled in unison.

"Well, somebody did! This time it wasn't a hang up! We have an actual voice on tape. Would you like to hear it?" Colburn asked.

"Damn straight," I said.

Mr. Colburn led us to a small room off the larger dispatch area. He found the tape in question, put it in a player and hit the button. We heard a voice, but just barely. The line was scratchy, the voice barely discernable. It could have been a man, a woman, or even a child. We heard the word "fire" and I could make out the voice saying, "upstairs . . . can't get out . . . help"—but that was all.

"Well, if we're having a cross-connection with someone else with the same model cordless telephone, Mr. Colburn, you realize that somebody is burned to death by now, don't you?" Willis said.

"We've gotten no further reports of a fire." Colburn looked at me. "Where were your children during all this, Mrs. Pugh?"

I'm not the violent type, but I did want to slug Mr. Colburn—right on his smug little kisser. "I was picking them up from school. Where they'd been all day. Without access to a telephone."

Willis moved very close to Mr. Colburn. "Look," he said, his voice low, dangerous, "my kids are not doing this. My kids do a lot of things, but they are not doing this. There is either a glitch in your system or in our telephone. I am taking the cordless tele-

phone out of commission and returning it to the store
where I bought it. If this happens again, I will assume it is the responsibility of the city, and we will
therefore expect compensation for my broken front
door. Do we understand each other, Mr. Colburn?"

Without waiting for Colburn's reply, Willis took
me by the arm and marched me out of the Emergency Services Center. Once in the parking lot, I
looked up at my husband and said, "You want me
here in the parking lot or do I have to wait until we
get home?"

We drove to Willis's mother's house where we'd
stashed the kids on our way to Colburn's. We went
in the kitchen door and my mother-in-law, Vera,
poured us both cups of coffee from the always-hot
coffeepot.

Sitting at her kitchen table, Vera said, "I know
Johnny Colburn. His mama's in my Sunday school
class. You just let me have a little talk with Mildred
Colburn. If anybody can straighten that boy out, it'll
be Mildred." She sighed. "It's all them newfangled
gadgets. Back in my day, you had a nice, simple,
plain black telephone with a dial. You didn't have to
listen to moozac 'cause nobody put you on hold and
you didn't have to figure out which button to push
with them damned electric voices talking in your ear.
I hate that."

"This is the craziest thing that's happened lately,"
I said, sipping at my coffee. Willis left to go in the
other room and start gathering the kids together. Not
too long ago it would have been me doing that, as
sittin' a spell with my mother-in-law would have
been unheard of. But the trouble with the Lesters last
year did something positive to my relationship with
Vera. We might not ever be bosom buddies—our age
difference and outlooks would keep that from hap-

pening—but we could spend time together now, and even shared a secret or two from Willis.

"Girl, you find out who hurt Megan with that Hershey's Kiss?"

I shook my head. "No, ma'am. We reported it to the cops and told the neighbors to be on the lookout, but nothing else like that's happened."

"Well, it's a crying shame when a child can't play in her own backyard! What this world is coming to, I swear to God!"

I sighed. "Vera, I think it was that boy next door. Brad McLemore?"

"The one dresses so stupid?"

"Yeah." I shook my head. "I shouldn't be saying that. I have no proof at all—"

"Nowadays, seems teenagers don't got a lick of sense," Vera said. "It's the music. That rap stuff. Why, we had a speaker in my Sunday school class not a month ago reading the words to some of them rap songs and he had to go 'beep' like every other word, they was so nasty! My Sunday school class is thinking about joining this Christian movement to have that kinda music banned from the radio and the record stores!" She beamed at me.

See? Outlook. Censorship is not something I could or would endorse. But if I told her so, we'd get into a twenty-minute argument and both end up mad, accomplishing nothing. I just kissed her on the forehead, thanked her for watching the kids, and went to find Willis.

We headed back to Black Cat Ridge. Ginger McLemore was standing in her driveway when we pulled into ours. Five-foot-five and slender, she had perfect blond hair in a perfect wedge cut that swung with silky abandon with each step. With even features and a pert little nose, she looked like every TV sitcom mom ever cast. Ginger was wearing pressed and starched khaki slacks (a perfect size nine) secured by an alligator skin belt, a cream-colored silk blouse with a cream-colored angora sweater thrown casually over her shoulders. Her jewelry was gold and dignified. Just the right size and amount of opulence for lounging around one's driveway. Her feet were clad in brown alligator flats that matched the belt. Donna Reed didn't die, she just moved in next door to me.

"My goodness," she said, smiling as we piled out of the car, "you had some excitement, didn't you?"

"False alarm," Willis said.

"When will you be fixing that front door?" she asked.

"Tomorrow," Willis answered.

Ginger sighed in apparent relief. "Oh, good," she said. "I was hoping it wouldn't take long. It's really an eyesore, you know." Then she whispered, "Property values."

"But we're all okay," I said. "Thanks for asking." I took my kids and marched into the house.

"That was rude," Willis said once we were inside.

"She certainly was."

"I meant you."

I shooed the kids upstairs, Graham to pretend he was doing his homework, Megan and Bessie to find new terrors to put Barbie and Ken through.

"*I* was rude?" I demanded.

Willis stretched out on the couch, remote control in his hand. "Well, so was she, but you didn't have to stoop to her level." He flicked the TV to life.

"I didn't stoop," I said, heading for the kitchen. "I kept my head high at all times."

No mail arrived the next day. As I was expecting a royalty check, the mail was something that held keen interest for me, and I might have noticed if Doug Kingsley wasn't there helping Willis hang the front door. It was a warmer than usual March day—

which necessitated Doug taking his shirt off. Hey—
we have the same rules, Willis and I. I can look too.

It took half the morning, what with going into
town to buy the door, then measuring and finding
out the door was too small. (When I suggested they
might have measured *before* they actually bought the
door, I got a long, drawn-out explanation about an
engineer's ability to "eye-ball" something so simple;
pointing out that "eye-balling" hadn't worked in this
case garnered me a glare and my husband's back for
almost an hour.) There was an argument between
Willis and Doug ("heated discussion," Willis insisted
it be called) about which side of the door was up
and, when that was solved, which side of the door
opened inward. I hung around supplying Doug (and
Willis, if he asked politely) with drinks and snacks.

Later that afternoon Willis and I took the disman-
tled cordless phone back to the hardware store where
it had originally been purchased and replaced it with
another brand.

The mail didn't come the next day either. Or the
day after that. I needed to get back to work; I had a
deadline on *Reflections in Turquoise*. On Thursday, I
finally talked myself into going back into my cubbyhole of an office, but before I turned on the computer,
I got a little manic. Finding the Fantastic under the
sink in the kitchen, I got a wet rag and sprayed it
with the cleanser, then set about cleaning each and
every key on the keyboard, the screen, the modem,
and the printer. To top off my mania, I cleaned the
outside of my file cabinets. Someone had been in my
office, obviously, putting the filth on my computer.
But even after the cleansing frenzy, it took a lot to
put my fingers on the keyboard, to boot up the system, to bring up the chapter I needed to work on—
the one where the smut had been added. But it was
clear now. It stopped where I had originally left it.

No one had added anything new since I'd erased the earlier mess.

I halfheartedly worked on getting Branson and Lavana into each other's arms, but I kept finding plot reasons to keep them out. I was delighted when my little alarm clock went off, telling me it was time to pick the kids up from school.

On Friday, two neighbors came over at different times bringing me bits and pieces of mail that hadn't been delivered the two days previous. As we live outside the city limits of Codderville, everyone in Black Cat Ridge has curbside mail service, which inspires a lot of terminally cute mailboxes. We have mailboxes in the shape of roosters, mailboxes with bluebonnets painted all over them, mailboxes sitting on miniature flagpoles and butter churns, mailboxes in cow patterns, mailboxes that look like little chateaux or cottages with thatched roofs. You name it, the subdivision has it—or will run out and get one just like it. I suppose our neighbors think we're a little on the dull side as ours is a plain black metal box on a plain black metal pole. And plainly empty for the past three days.

The mail delivery was anytime Delbert Busch felt like coming out our way. Sometimes mornings, sometimes afternoons—I was never sure. But he was always good about giving people the right mail. I called the post office in Codderville to see if maybe someone else was delivering in place of Delbert. Maybe he was on vacation or sick. But no, Delbert was fine. I explained the situation and they said they'd look into it.

That afternoon neighbors a block over—three different neighbors, none of whom I'd ever met—brought me more mail. My royalty check was not among the proffered items.

When the mail finally did start arriving, there were

four letters in there from men who were answering my personals ad.

"Someone is harassing me," I told Luna on the phone.

"Uh-huh," she said, obviously doing something else and not paying that much attention to me.

"Are you listening to me?" I demanded.

"Someone's harassing you," she said.

"Yes. I'm beginning to think those 911 calls were rigged somehow."

"How?" she demanded.

"I don't know! There's all sorts of electronic gadgetry out now."

"You have a high-tech stalker, huh?"

One of the letters had said that the man was answering my ad from the *Houston Post.* Another from the *Austin American-Statesman.* I'd called both papers and had them fax a copy of both ads to Willis's fax machine. He'd called an hour before barely able to contain himself he'd been laughing so hard.

"They're both the same ad. Okay, are you ready?" he'd asked, giggling.

"Just shut up and read it," I said between clinched teeth.

"Hey, fella, looking for a good time? Well-endowed MWF looking for any man, any time, any way. Likes hot food, hot showers, and hot sex." Willis could barely get the words out he was laughing so hard.

"Did you do this?" I demanded.

That sobered him up. "Me? Jesus, why would I advertise you?"

"Because you think it's so funny. Maybe you thought you'd play a little joke on ol' E.J.?"

"Eej, I wouldn't do that. I swear. Honey, look. It's a harmless prank—"

"Just like the 911 calls and the mail disappearing?

What about the harmless glass in the chocolate, Willis? And the vile filth on my computer?"

"Are you accusing me of hurting my child, Eloise?"

"No, of course not. I know none of this is your style. Except for the ad."

"Well, I didn't put the damn ad in the paper, okay?"

I sighed. "I know, honey. I'm sorry. This whole thing just has me so shook up—"

Everybody thought it was funny. Luna had laughed like an idiot when I read her the ad. The letters answering the ad, however, weren't that funny. There were sick people in the world, and two out of the four letters were from them. I read Luna the letters. Basically, these two gentlemen's ideas of love were a little on the painful-sounding side.

"Look, E.J., if you know who's doing this, then I'll do something about it. But until you find out who it is, there's nothing much I can do," Luna said.

It was on the tip of my tongue to suggest she check out Brad McLemore, but I couldn't bring myself to do it. He was a pathetic little shit, but not necessarily felonious.

"Can't you investigate?" I asked. "Find out who's doing it?"

"How?"

"Call the papers! Find out who put the ad in there!"

"All right."

"You'll do it?" I couldn't believe my ears. She was going to actually do something.

"Yes, I'll do it. But I can tell you right now what they'll say."

"What's that?" I asked, my heart sinking. No one says that line unless the next one was either bad or useless.

"That the ads were paid for by either cash or a money order and either no return address or a mail drop."

I sighed. "Just check it out for me, okay?"

"Sure," she said. "Meanwhile, keep your doors and windows locked and your car doors, too."

"Yeah, right."

"E.J.?" she said.

"What?"

"Does Willis like hot food too?" She giggled and hung up.

Two more days and my royalty check still hadn't arrived. I finally called my agent.

"When did you mail the check, Glennis?"

"Well over a week ago," my agent said in her phony British accent. Her name was really Glenda Anne Sumner, but she'd changed it to Glennis Summers twenty years before when she'd left Valdosta, Georgia, for New York. The British accent came and went, interspersed with her version of a New Zealand accent, but she'd been my agent for all eight years of my romance-writing career, and her business sense was what I was paying for, not her sense of style.

I explained the situation with my mail. "It's possible the check was stolen," I finally said. "Can you trace it through your bank? Put a stop payment on it?"

"Certainly, darling. I'm just devastated this is happening to you!"

"You and me both. Call me and let me know what the bank says."

I rang off and sat staring at my kitchen curtains, blowing in the slight breeze from the open window. When the breeze got a little stronger, the curtains blew up enough for me to view the driveway between our house and the McLemores. Brad was standing there. Staring at my house.

Luna called that afternoon to give me her version of "I told you so."

"I called both the *Post* and the *Statesman*," she said.

"Uh-huh," I said, resigned.

"Both ads were paid for in cash. The name and address given was yours."

"It just makes me feel all warm and fuzzy inside knowing these sicko perverts who wrote those letters know my address."

"Move," Luna suggested.

I grunted a response worthy of my husband and hung up.

Conner came over to play later that afternoon. Graham had gone to the store with his father but was due back any minute. I asked Conner to come on in and wait for Graham. He sat at the kitchen table and watched as I started dinner.

"You must be a very good cook, Mrs. Pugh," he said, smiling that perfect Eddie Haskell smile.

"What makes you say that, Conner?"

"Because your home always smells so wonderful!"

I worked at producing a smile, reminding myself he was only eight years old. That, of course, made me wonder how bad he'd be at sixteen.

"So," I said, getting down to the only reason I let him wait for Graham, rather than come back later, "how's your brother?"

The smile left Conner's face and his eyes widened in surprise. "Brad?" he asked.

I laughed. "How many brothers do you have?"

"Just Brad. He's more than enough." Conner frowned. "Why do you want to know about Brad, Mrs. Pugh?"

"Just idle curiosity, Conner."

He smiled. "Well, he's just fine. Thank you for asking."

"Is he still going to school full time?"

"Yes. Why do you ask?"

I smiled, copying Conner's own enigmatic smile. "No reason." I wanted to say, of course, that I wondered about school because Brad seemed to be staring at my house when he should have been staring out a school room window. That Brad seemed to be home a lot more often than he should be and in their driveway a lot more often than I wanted. But I didn't say any of that. Maybe I could say it to the mother, but not to an eight-year-old boy.

Graham finally returned with his father and the boys went upstairs to play. Two hours later there was a knock at the back door. I asked Willis to get it. I figured it was Brad McLemore coming to pick up Conner. I really didn't want to look at him right then.

Four

On Monday morning, UPS delivered a package. Or, I should say, box. It was so big the UPS man had to bring it inside and deposit it in the foyer. I thanked him, showed him out, then spent precious minutes staring at the box. That's when I called Luna.

"UPS just delivered a great big box to my front door."

"That's nice," she said. "Is it your birthday?"

"No, it isn't," I said. "Neither is it from Santa Claus, the Easter Bunny, or the tooth fairy. I think, however, it might be a bomb."

"Why?" she asked, her voice sharp.

"Why not?" I demanded.

"Is it ticking?" she asked.

"Do they still do that? I thought with plastique and all this new stuff, ticking wasn't a sure sign of anything any more."

"That's true." She was silent for a moment. Finally I heard her sigh. "Don't touch it," she said.

"I have no intention—"

"I'll be there in fifteen minutes with a member of the bomb squad."

She was true to her word—except it was more like seventeen and a half minutes; but who's counting? The man with her, whom she introduced as Manny Espinoza, the only member of Codderville PD who'd taken the bomb class from the Austin Police Department, asked us to leave the house while he checked out the box.

Luna and I gathered up the cats and headed into the backyard. Ten minutes later, Officer Espinoza invited us back into the house. The box was standing open and I noticed Officer Espinoza looking anywhere but at me. Luna and I went to it and looked inside. Well, there wasn't a bomb. There were, however, sex toys. Lots and lots of sex toys. Whips and chains, handcuffs, black leather-studded dog collars, dildos in all shapes and sizes, crotchless panties, bras with the nipples cut out, and a few things I neither recognized nor cared to ponder their use.

I've never considered myself a prude. Although I've only had sex with one man my entire life (Willis), we've done our share of experimentation. But the extent of our kinkiness has been whipped cream. My stomach heaved at the sight of the contents of the box, reminding me of the words written on my computer screen. I went to my office and brought the printed pages out, handing them to Luna while explaining how they had appeared on my screen.

She read the pages and looked at me. "Did you ever read *Sybil*?" she asked.

I rolled my eyes. "Yes. And no—I don't have MPS. Willis would have noticed."

"What's PMS have to do with it?" she asked.

"Not PMS, MPS—multiple personality syndrome."

"I knew that," she said. "It was just a thought." She began perusing the printed pages, then looked again at the contents of the box. "There seems to be a pattern here. This filth," she said, waving the pages, "the sex toys. The suggestive ad in the newspapers." She looked at me. "You wink at any guys lately?"

"Oh, right, Luna, turn it on the victim! No, I haven't winked at any guys lately." I sighed. It was time to talk about Brad McLemore.

Officer Espinoza had come in a separate car. He told Luna he'd see her back at the office and left. I took Luna into the kitchen and poured us both iced teas. Checking the clock, I saw that I had plenty of time before I needed to go pick up the kids from school.

We sat down at the kitchen table and I told her about Brad: about him telling me he'd read one of my books, about the time alone in the house while we were at the hospital with Megan, only days before I discovered the filth on my computer screen. About someone having messed with my jewelry, about Brad hanging around too much, staring at the house.

"I'll check him out," she said when I'd finished.

"I don't want problems with the neighbors, Luna. Be discreet, huh?"

She grinned. "When have you ever known me to be less than discreet?"

I walked her to the front door. "This is going to blow up in my face, isn't it? You're going to charge in there and accuse the kid of all sorts of things—"

The phone rang. Luna waved and walked out the door. The call was from Glennis, my agent, telling me the check had been cashed. I figured I knew what the money had been spent on and that the bounty was now in a big box on my foyer floor. I put the phone down thinking that now maybe I'd get some action—mail theft being a federal offense and all.

"So what are we going to do now?" Willis demanded. "We need that money!"

"Willis, it's like I had cash in my purse and somebody stole it. We're responsible. It's not Glennis's fault."

"The house insurance would cover that, won't it?"

We'd been dropped by our former insurance company the year before because of all the claims due to the fire and other problems resulting from the murder of the Lesters, and now we were insured through a company called Insurance Are Us, or something equally generic. The premiums were sky high and the items they didn't cover took an entire page of the policy.

"I doubt it," I told him.

Willis threw himself down on the couch and sighed mightily. "Well, this is just wonderful," he said.

"Honey—"

He sat up. "You know we need that money! We count on that money twice a year!"

I gave my husband *the look*. "Just how were you planning on spending *my* money?" I demanded.

Willis looked away from me. "Never mind," he said.

"Willis."

He finally faced at me. "Well, Doug and I found this really great deal on a twenty-four-foot fiberglass boat. Used but in really good condition. We thought we'd go halves—"

I turned and walked into the kitchen, looking at the old refrigerator I'd planned to replace with my royalty check. I started dinner.

That night I had the dream again, the one where we're having a backyard barbecue with the Lesters.

There's a tree that hangs over the fence from the neighbor's house behind us. In the spring it's full of beautiful white blossoms. Terry and I are sitting in lawn chairs under the overhanging branches laughing at Roy and Willis wearing stupid chef's hats and fencing with their long-handled spatulas. Butterflies, fifty or more, flit from branch to branch of the tree. The kids are playing, the boys running around chasing the butterflies, the little girls playing with Barbies. Monique is on the cordless phone we'd just taken back to the store, talking to a boy.

I woke up with tears in my eyes. I always do. I have three sisters, but I'd never felt as close to any of them as I had to Terry Lester. Willis was snoring in the bed next to me. I gently removed his arm from my waist and slid out of bed, heading downstairs for a glass of ice water.

I pride myself on my night vision. I rarely turn a light on when walking through the house late at night since I know where everything is and usually have no problems. Willis, however, can't walk through a totally empty room in the dark without tripping over something. I didn't turn on any lights as I walked barefoot into the kitchen. A movement on the driveway that separated our house from the McLemores' caught my eye. I went to the breakfast room window and looked out. Arthur McLemore's black Lexus was pulling out of the driveway with the car lights off. And the man in the front seat was definitely Arthur.

"Where in the world is he going in the middle of the night?" I thought, shrugging to myself in the way one does when one really doesn't give a damn.

As I turned toward the kitchen I noticed the drapes that covered the sliding glass door that looked out over our backyard had been left open. As I reached to close them I saw Brad McLemore standing in the backyard—inside our *fenced* backyard. I moved quickly behind the drapes, hoping he hadn't seen me. He must not have. He didn't move. He stood like a statue, staring up at my bedroom window.

"I talked to Brad," Luna said. "He doesn't know anything about anything he says."

"You expected him to spill his guts?" I asked.

"I'll admit the kid's a little off," Luna said, "but I doubt he has the brains to pull off most of what's been going on with you."

"He was staring at my bedroom window in the middle of the night!"

"Doesn't mean he's anything more than a Peeping Tom."

"Oh, for Christ's sake!" I slammed the phone down. I knew I'd have to go by the bank on my way to pick up the kids. I owed the "cussing" kitty about four dollars and some change.

Twenty minutes later I went out to my car to go get the kids from school. Brad McLemore was standing in the driveway, not even pretending anymore to be shooting hoops.

I walked straight up to him. "I know you've been doing this," I said, gritting my teeth. "I saw you last night in my backyard. You do that again, I'll have you arrested for trespassing. You don't come over to my house for any reason, do you understand me? Conner can go home on his own or Willis will walk him home. You don't come near me or my kids again or I'll have your ass in jail, do you understand me?"

He shook his head, rolling his eyes and sneering. "Jeez, who'd wanna look at a fat old cow like you, anyway?"

He turned and walked into the house. I got in the car and drove to my kids' school.

The tree from my dream of the night before was beginning to bloom for real in the backyard. The butterflies were there, as they were every year. I watched from the kitchen window as Megan and Bessie tried to jump up to the overhanging branches, trying to reach a blossom or a butterfly—who knew? Graham and Conner were upstairs in Graham's room, doing God only knew what. The phone rang. I picked it up.

"Hello?"

"Did you like your present?" The voice was metallic, hardly human.

"Who is this?" I demanded.

"Your friend," the voice said. "The friend that leaves you little gifts. Do you like my gifts, E.J.?"

I hung up the phone quickly. My hands were trembling. I went to the door and called the girls inside. Yes, it was a pretty day, yes it was warm outside. No, you can't play out there anymore. Maybe never again. I hugged them to me, feeling their body heat, smelling the child sweat.

"Mommy!" Bessie said, pulling away. "You hug too hard!" I smiled down at her. It was only the second time she'd called me mommy. She usually called me nothing at all. The sound of that turned the cold inside me from the call to warmth.

And it made me mad. I had three kids who'd been through hell less than a year before. I'd been through hell myself. And now someone was trying to do it again. I wouldn't let it happen. I looked at the two sweat-shiny faces looking up at me, Megan with her strawberry blond hair and blue eyes, already tall for her age, and petite Bessie with her dark brown curly tresses and her cocker spaniel brown eyes. I wouldn't let anything bad touch them again.

"We have to get rid of it," I told Willis as we stared at the box in the garage, the box filled with sex toys.

"Garage sale?" my husband suggested.

I gave him the look. "Burn them. Give them to Doug. He's single. Just get them off the property. Graham could figure out what all this stuff is, you know that, don't you?"

Willis picked up a strange metal device, long and thin, with a protruding shoehorn-type apparatus on the end with a hole in the center. "Graham could probably explain to us what this is," Willis said. "Maybe we should take them back to a sex shop. Get some of that royalty check money back."

I walked to the open door of the garage. "Fine," I said. "You go. Leave me out of it."

Willis brandished the handcuffs. "You sure we can't keep just these?"

Ignoring him I walked toward the house. I heard the McLemores' back door open and close. Afraid to look, afraid it was Brad, I kept walking toward our gate.

"E.J.?"

The voice was female. I turned to see Ginger McLemore prettily leaping the foot-high picket fence that separated the driveways. Today it was pearls and a cotton sweater the exact color of her hair over a multicolored broomstick skirt. Her nails were freshly manicured and her makeup was better than mine had been at my wedding.

I walked back to meet her. "Hi, Ginger," I said.

The look on her face was the one she wore while officiating as the president of the elementary school PTA. "The police questioned Brad about some problems you're having?" she asked, a butter-wouldn't-melt-in-her-mouth smile on her face.

"Brad's been staring in my windows at night, Ginger."

Ginger's perfect face developed a frown. "Oh, my goodness, E.J. That's just terrible. But it can't have been Brad."

"Why?"

"Brad doesn't go out at night," she said. She smiled. Her smile seemed to say, *There. That settles that.*

"Ginger, I saw him last night, around two A.M., inside my fenced backyard. I have very good vision and there was a light burning in the backyard. It was Brad."

Ginger smiled sweetly. "No, I don't think so."

My head was beginning to ache from the strain of talking with this woman. "Ginger," I said, my voice rising in spite of myself, "this isn't opinion—it's fact! I saw him with my own eyes."

She reached out a tiny hand and gently squeezed my arm. "Brad was home in bed all night last night, E.J."

"How do you know that?" I demanded. "Do you sleep in his room?"

I felt the gentle restraining arm of my husband across my shoulders. "Ginger, we're really sorry about all this, but some really unusual things have been happening lately," Willis said. He smiled. "We're not saying Brad is responsible, but we feel under the circumstances, with the glass-laced candy Megan got into—"

Ginger actually laughed. "Why, I can't even fathom for a moment that you would think Brad capable of something like that! Why, he just adores children. Look at the relationship he and Conner have. A mother couldn't ask for two closer or happier little boys." Talk about your Queen of De Nile, I thought. Again she touched my arm. "I would think with your *liberal* bent you wouldn't judge Brad just because of his silly clothes, E.J."

"I'm not, Ginger," I said, getting really pissed now. I mean, she actually used the *l*-word. "I'm judging him by the fact that he was trespassing in my backyard in the middle of the night!"

"Ladies, please," Willis said.

I turned and glared at him. Willis shrugged and went back into the garage.

"Just keep Brad away from our house, Ginger. That's all I ask—"

"But he's never been near your house, E.J. Except to pick up Conner, of course." She smiled sweetly, turned, and walked back to her house. That I didn't run after her and snatch her baldheaded shows what a really big *l*-word I truly am.

I hugged closer to Willis in the bed, the curve of his back and his really great buns nestled up next to me, my arms around his arms, my chin on his shoulder. "What do we do now?" I asked, my breath moving the tiny hairs on his back.

"I dunno, babe," he said, staring at the far wall. "I guess we could get the phone number changed." His arm, which had been hanging at his side, moved back to rub my hip. I began to think he wasn't all that interested in my scary phone call.

"How about moving?" I whispered.

His head came up and he turned his body towards me, dislodging our great spoon position. "Sell the house?" By his tone I might have said rent out the children.

"Yeah. And move to Cleveland. Or Buffalo." I sighed and turned, reversing our spoon. "All I know is I'm not sure how much more I can take."

I felt his hot breath in my ear. "You know, of course," I said, "that those phony 911 calls were rigged?"

"What makes you say that?" he asked, his hand pulling up my nightgown and stroking my thigh.

"Everything else that's going on. It just stands to reason. Too much of a coincidence not to be . . . oh, yes, right there."

"You're probably right," he said, pulling my gown

off over my head, "but I don't think I want to discuss it further right at the moment."

Needless to say, we didn't. Discuss it further, I mean.

It was a typical Monday morning. Graham couldn't find his math homework, which he swore he'd done. We had to take his room apart and discovered it finally under his aquarium. The math homework, of course, was only half finished.

Megan, who's now in a separate class from Bessie (on the advice of our family therapist who thought the girls could use some away-time from each other), informed me she was supposed to have thirty-five cupcakes for school that day. Bessie, the angel, refused to eat her Cheerios and threw the bowl of milk and cereal on the floor in an unusual display of temper. It took an extra ten minutes to make her clean it up herself. The family therapist said that was the only way to make Bessie be a part of the family: to treat her as badly as I do my other children. We were now in the process of legally adopting Bessie, so we're back in therapy to deal with that. Life is a process, and it's amazing how expensive that process can be when your insurance doesn't cover it.

Bert had a seizure and Ernie, in sympathy I suppose, threw up on the carpet in the dining room. Bessie started crying because her cat was sick and Megan (the most sentimental of all children) demanded a refund on Bert.

"Can't we take him back and get a cat that doesn't shake?" she asked.

"Bert's special, sweetheart. He's got a problem and we love him all the more because of it."

"Maybe *you* do," she said.

Like I said, a typical Monday morning. All I could think about was getting the little buggers off to school and spending six whole hours by myself.

Branson and Lavana needed me if they were ever to consummate their miserable relationship. And, besides, I had a Mars Bar hidden in the shelf on top of the refrigerator. I can usually keep my chocolate addiction under control, but with all that had been happening lately, I figured it beat the hell out of straight gin.

Needless to say I was not happy when I finally got everybody out to the car. I was even less happy when I opened the door of the backseat to let the kids in and found Brad McLemore's nude, and decidedly dead, body lying there.

Five

There's something to be said for a Rubenesque figure. Since the kids were behind me, my ample girth was enough to block their view of the body lying on the backseat of the car. I used my butt to move them back further and firmly shut the door. Turning to Graham, I said, "Take your sisters inside the house and bring me the cordless phone. Immediately."

I guess enough bad things had happened in Graham's young life that he had learned to respond to a certain tone in my voice in an uncharacteristic manner. He did as he was told. And when I added, "Quickly," he actually scurried, pushing his little sisters in front of him like an usher with late arrivals only seconds before the house lights dimmed.

When he came out carrying the cordless phone, he simply said, "Who is it?"

I decided to cry about my eight-year-old son's lost innocence at another time. I said, "Brad."

Graham looked at me, shook his head, and went back inside the house. Deciding not to take the chance of dialing 911, I called Luna's direct line instead. She answered on the second ring.

"Luna—" I started.

"I have someone at my desk right now, may I call you back?"

"I have a dead body in my car. So call me." I hung up and leaned against the closed back door of the station wagon.

The phone in my hand rang. "Yes?"

"If this is a joke, I *will* arrest your ass, be assured of that." Luna's voice was not pleasant.

"I think we don't need to worry about Brad McLemore harassing me anymore," I said.

"Please don't tell me you killed him."

"No, I didn't. But his mother is right next door and I would rather you be the one to tell her that her son's nude body is lying on the backseat of my car—"

"I told you to always lock your car doors, didn't I tell you that? I'm on my way."

I hung up the phone and laid it on the roof of the car. I kept my back to the thing inside the station wagon. *Not again*, my mind screamed. *Please, God, not again.* I'd had my share of finding dead bodies last year—more than anyone's share of finding the dead bodies of children. Even if he had the body of a grown man, Brad McLemore had still been a child. Now he was a dead child. I'd read somewhere that, statistically speaking, men between the ages of sixteen and twenty-five had more of a chance of being killed now than they did during the Vietnam era. There was no statistic anywhere that said overweight, redheaded housewives had to be the ones to find them.

Turning, I forced myself to carefully open the back door and looked inside. Brad McLemore was lying

on his back, one leg on the seat of the car, the other
falling to the floor. Both hands were across his chest,
as if arranged. His head was leaning back at an angle,
and his coloring, to say the least, was not good. It
had a blueish-gray tinge to it and a blueish tongue
was protruding between his teeth. His neck, exposed
due to the angle of his head, was heavily discolored,
with bruising in a straight horizontal line about an
inch in width. Curiously enough, there were two
deeper lines of bruising within the width, about a
quarter inch apart. It didn't take Quincy to figure out
Brad McLemore had been strangled with some sort
of cord or rope. My mind absorbed this in a clinically
detached way. My stomach, however, wasn't so detached. I slammed the door of the wagon, took two
steps to my oleander bushes and heaved up my
Cheerios.

Luna arrived minutes later, followed by a patrol
car and an ambulance. I was afraid all the activity
would bring Ginger McLemore out for a look-see,
and I wasn't wrong. She opened her back door and
peered out.

I nudged Luna. "That's his mother," I said.

Luna turned and looked at Ginger. "Okay."

I went in the house to see to my children. I knew
Luna would be able to find me when she needed me.
I didn't want to be out there when Ginger McLemore
saw her son.

The kids were upstairs watching TV in the master
bedroom, the girls delirious about an extra day off
from school, and I was seriously contemplating the
dust bunnies under the easy chair from my perch on
the sofa when Luna walked in the back door.

"Pugh?" she shouted.

"In the living room," I called back.

She walked in and stood in the doorway, arms

akimbo. "I think we should start calling you Jessica Fletcher."

"You know, I have a theory that when that show finally ends we're going to discover that Jessica Fletcher is the most cunning, devious serial killer in American history and that there are thousands of people on death rows all across the country who were unwittingly duped into confessing to crimes she actually committed—"

"You're babbling, Pugh."

I sighed. "Yes, I suppose you're right." An involuntary shudder wracked my body. "I had this silly hope that the next dead body I encountered would be my own, fifty-odd years from now."

Luna came and sat down next to me on the couch, touching my arm lightly with her hand. "You okay?"

"He was just a baby, Luna. The same age as Monique—"

She squeezed my arm. "Tell me what happened."

I shook my head, trying to dislodge the image of Brad's swollen, blueish face. "I opened the car door to put the kids in the backseat to take them to school and there he was."

"Did you hear anything last night?"

I shook my head.

"See anything?"

I shook my head. "Did you tell Ginger?" I asked.

"Yeah. She's in her house now calling her husband."

"How'd she take it?"

Luna shrugged. "A real trooper. Hardly fainted at all when she saw her son's naked body lying there."

I heard steps on the stairs and looked over my shoulder to the stairway. Graham stood there. I motioned for him to come and he came and sat next to me, nestling himself under my arm. We hadn't sat like that since Graham was two or three. It felt good, but I wasn't really sure who was comforting whom.

"Is Brad really dead?" he asked.

My fingers trailed through his dark reddish hair and I said, "Yes, honey. I'm sorry."

He buried his head in my side, I suppose to hide the tears from Luna and myself.

Luna massaged my shoulder with her hand for a quick second, then patted my back. "Gotta go."

"I hate this shit," Willis said. "I really, really hate this shit."

"Fifty cents," I said.

"What?" he demanded.

"You owe the cussing kitty fifty cents."

We sat in the living room. I'd fed the kids lunch and sent them back upstairs. There was some grumbling from the girls about what a pretty day it was outside and why couldn't they go out and play since they weren't sick, but Graham, sweet Graham, grabbed them both by the scruff of the neck and announced if they didn't shut up he wouldn't let them in his room to see his stuff. As this would be the first time they'd been so honored, they clammed up and headed for the stairs.

"Did you hear anything last night?" I asked my husband, not unaware that I was echoing Luna's questions from earlier in the day.

"No."

"See anything?"

Willis stretched out on the couch, putting his shoes on the arm like he wasn't supposed to do. "Well, sure, I saw this big burly guy carrying a body and shoving it into the backseat of our car, but I didn't think anything about it." He rolled his eyes. He's never been what one might call the king of sarcasm. Whereas I, of course, am the queen.

"Are you going back to work?"

"Ha," he said, picking up the remote control. "And

leave you alone? You might find another dead body."

The next day was relatively normal for a nineties family reduced to only one vehicle. The station wagon, as the second-to-final resting place of Brad McLemore, had been impounded by the police. I convinced Willis he should take the kids to school on his way to work, which would make him only a little over an hour late. Graham was quiet that morning, uncharacteristically quiet. I asked him if he wanted to stay home from school, but he said no. Was murder becoming so commonplace to my son, like snow days up north, that it didn't even deserve a day off from school? We hadn't told the girls yet about Brad. I didn't know how to do that. They weren't close to Brad, I reasoned. They might not notice he was gone. Then again, they were sure to find out. Conner McLemore went to the same school. There'd be talk. I had to tell them. Again. Again I had to tell my children about the death of another child.

With Willis taking the kids to school with the only remaining car, I would be homebound, but, when you write for a living, there are worse things to be. I called a homeroom mother I knew and made arrangements for the kids to be brought home in the afternoon, then I made a heaping pot of my famous chicken paprika, halved it, putting one half in my best casserole dish. I went upstairs and put on my good denim skirt and one of Willis's Oxford cloth shirts I'd inherited and some flats and took the chicken paprika over to the McLemores' house.

I rang the doorbell, totally unsure of what kind of reception to expect. Ginger opened the door. "Ginger," I said, "I brought you some food. I'm so sorry—"

Ginger smiled brightly. "Oh, how sweet. Please come in." She held the door open for me. Being the nasty creature I am, I checked the place out thoroughly. It was a cream-colored couch, so Graham was right about "sorta white." The room looked like a decorator's dream, not a home in which to raise two young boys.

"I'm so sorry about Brad—"

Ginger took the proffered covered dish from my hands. "It must have been awful for you, discovering him and all," Ginger said, leading the way into the kitchen. She put my dish down with the dozen or so other covered dishes lining the countertops. Ginger had obviously been sitting at the kitchen table. There was a coffee cup and an open magazine on the table.

"How are you holding up?" I asked.

She smiled. "As well as can be expected. Arthur and I thought it best that we make things as normal as possible, so he went to work and dropped Conner off at school on the way."

"Conner's at school?" I couldn't quite hide my disbelief. His brother murdered the day before and they send the kid off to school? I hoped they'd told him, because if they hadn't, Graham was liable to. That would be an awful way to find out.

"He's very resilient," Ginger said, smiling that smile again. That smile I'd like to see forever in formaldehyde. Ginger threw her arms up in mock alarm. "Where are my manners? Would you like a cup of coffee?"

"Uh, sure. Fine. Let me get it—"

"No, no, now you just sit. You had a terrible ordeal yesterday. Let me get the coffee."

"I had a terrible ordeal? Ginger, for God's sake—"

"Cream and sugar or black?"

"Black, one sugar," I said, sighing.

She brought the coffees and sat down again across from me. Was this shock? Or was this the most bizarre woman I'd ever met? "It's so sweet of you to come over here like this, E.J.," she said. "I know we haven't been the best of friends, but I certainly hope that will change."

I doubted it. Most of my friends were sane. "That would be nice," I said a trifle weakly. I took a big gulp of my coffee, burning my tongue and my throat and almost spitting it across the table.

Ginger patted my shoulder. "Are you all right?"

"Yes, fine," I said. "Uh, about the funeral?"

"Oh, we're members of the Black Cat Ridge Church of the Brethren, do you know it?"

I knew *of* it. A fundamentalist sect out of Houston that had bought up about three hundred acres for a retreat out here in the boonies. The leader of the flock flew in on Sundays in his Lear jet, landing it on the private airstrip of the retreat grounds. I nodded my head.

"Well, the service will be this Saturday at the church, and the burial will be on the grounds. I hope you and your family will be able to come?" she asked brightly, like some people ask about your attendance at an upcoming barbecue.

I almost said, "We'd be delighted," but choked off my words to say, "Of course."

"E.J., I have an etiquette question for you."

"Yes?"

"Well, first of all, let me tell you that Arthur and I tried for several years to have a child of our own, but the Lord didn't bless us that way, so when a young girl in the church we belonged to in Houston got pregnant, well, we knew her parents and the boy's parents, so we knew what good Christian families they came from, and children will make mistakes, you know, so we agreed to adopt the baby. That was Brad, of course. And then, wouldn't you know it, seven years later, the Lord gives us our own baby! Why, you could've just knocked me over with a feather when the doctor told me I was pregnant with Conner, I was that shocked. But, my etiquette question is: Should I notify the birth families about Brad's death? I thought maybe they'd like to attend the funeral. What do you think?"

That was certainly one for Miss Manners. I had no earthly idea how to answer that and told Ginger so. I suggested she ask her pastor.

"What a wonderful idea! If I wasn't so distressed about all this, I probably would have thought of it myself!" She beamed at me to show her distress.

I'd had enough of the grieving Ginger. "I've got to go now," I said standing. "I have a dentist's appointment." It was a weak lie, but it was mine own.

Ginger stood with me, walking me to the back door. She laughed. "Don't you just hate that? Dentists are the worst. Everytime I go I think of Steve Martin in that movie—"

"*Little Shop of Horrors*," I supplied.

She laughed again. "Yes! That's it. What a funny movie! After we saw it the first time, Conner said he wanted to grow up to be a dentist! Why, Arthur and I just laughed and laughed!"

I'll just bet you did, I thought to myself. I smiled. "Well, hope you enjoy the chicken," I said, then scooted out the door as fast as possible.

"They're weird," I said into the phone. My audience was Willis's new secretary, Angel. Willis was in a meeting and I had to tell someone about my encounter with Ginger McLemore.

"The whole family sound like definite nut cases," Angel agreed.

I sighed. "Maybe I'm being unfair. Maybe it's some fundamentalist religious thing. Maybe she feels strongly that Brad's in a better place."

"Uh-huh," Angel said, obviously not buying it. "Or maybe she's weird."

I sighed. "This whole thing reminds me of my Aunt Deliah's new puppy," I said.

"Okay," Angel said, "you have my attention. How is this like your Aunt Deliah's new puppy?"

"Well, she and Uncle Joe had this old dog for years, Mutt, his name was. Then one of my cousins gave my Aunt Deliah this registered beagle puppy and poor Mutt got relegated to the backyard. They hardly ever let him in the house anymore. I mean, they feed him and care for him, but that puppy is the be-all and end-all, know what I mean?"

"Ah. You think Brad was the apple of the McLemores' eye until their—excuse the expression—'real' child came along, then they basically ignored him for Conner?"

"It's a theory. The kid was a real mess. A loner. No friends. And that just isn't any kind of normal grieving Ginger McLemore's doing."

In a high singsong voice, Angel said, "Can you say dysfunctional family?"

"Wonder if Mr. Rogers would like to visit *my* neighborhood?" I said, laughing.

"You going to the funeral?" she asked.

"Probably. Wanna come?"

"Um, Saturday. That's the day I water the goldfish, I do believe."

"Chicken," I said and rang off.

It was the first week of April, and spring was springing with a vengeance. We hadn't had a cold snap in over a week. Trees were blossoming like crazy, and the bluebonnets on the sides of the road heading for the Brethren retreat were like a blanket of color. As we drove the five miles out of Black Cat Ridge into the country, we spotted family after family taking pictures of babies and children sitting in the bluebonnets, a Texas tradition. We had our own gallery in the upstairs hall of babies in bluebonnets, an annual picture, and we planned on taking more on the trip back from the funeral. It would be the first to include Bessie.

Thinking of what I'd told Angel about my aunt and uncle's new puppy made me wonder about my own ability to juggle my affection for my children. Did I love one more than the other? Had I been lavishing more affection on Bessie because of her newness and her tragic life? Did my children know they were loved? As we pulled into the gates of the retreat, I decided to push those disturbing questions aside for a later date (maybe some night when I felt it would be better to stay up worrying until all hours).

The Brethren retreat was something to see. The gate was manned and the funeral was by invitation only. We had ours and presented it to the guard. The main complex was a huge white rock affair, what some call the Austin Mission-look. White rock and metal roof with huge beams and joists seen from the front. We were directed by the guard, however, to go around that building to the chapel on Luke Road. As we passed different streets, we noticed they were all named for disciples: Matthew Avenue, John Way, Mark Circle, etc. Cute, I thought.

The chapel looked much older than the rest of the complex; built of dark red and brown rock, it seemed to have grown out of the very ground on which it stood. We parked our car with dozens of others in a lot across Luke Road from the chapel and entered. I don't believe in bringing very young children to funerals, but the invitation said there would be babysitting. We found the spot for that and sent the girls off to play. Graham had asked to attend. We'd agreed.

The three of us sat in the back of the church. I could see Ginger and Arthur and Conner McLemore up at the front. Conner leaned around his mother when we walked in and waved and grinned at Graham. Graham waved back. It was a long service and pretty jovial. There was a lot of singing and clapping, and when the preacher began to speak, a lot of "hallelujahs" were called out from the crowd of mourners. And the music wasn't the dreary sort we get at our Methodist church, but a mixture of old gospel songs and new semi-rock 'n' roll stuff.

All in all, except for the woman next to me who began to speak in tongues halfway through the service, it wasn't a bad funeral, although it felt more like an old-fashioned tent revival meeting than the sending off to glory of a teenaged boy. Very little was said about Brad. The pastor seemed to concentrate more on what upstanding citizens Ginger and Arthur were than on the fact that a sixteen-year-old boy had been murdered—senselessly ripped away from his family.

We followed the congregation across the road to the cemetery, which was relatively new, only as old as the retreat itself (about ten years), and wasn't terribly full. They'd picked a spot on a hill with towering live oaks to bury their dead. The McLemore family had a large plot edged in stone. The only grave in the family plot was the one into which they lowered Brad's casket after a brief graveside service.

As we were leaving the cemetery, we had to pass through a gate that was serving as a reception area. The McLemore family stood there greeting their guests. As we neared, Arthur McLemore embraced me, rocking me back and forth. When he finally let me go, he said, "I'm so sorry you had to find him like that. What a good neighbor you are!"

Well, that took me aback. Bringing in your mail while you're on vacation, feeding the dog, watering the plants, saying hello over the backyard fence—that was a good neighbor. I didn't see how discovering someone's dead son in my car deserved a gold star for good neighborliness.

We extracted ourselves from the "Happy Family"

and made our way out of the complex. A mile or two down the road, we stopped by a hill covered with bluebonnets and took our annual pictures. Each child was photographed separately, then paired, then all three together, then Mom and all, then Dad and all, until each combination had been exhausted. It was during the photo frenzy that it dawned on me that neither Ginger nor Arthur McLemore had mentioned wondering who might have murdered their son.

It just never seemed to come up.

It was later that day when there was a knock on the back door. I went and opened it to find Conner McLemore standing there.

"Hello, Mrs. Pugh," he said, smiling from ear to ear. "How nice to see you again. It was very kind of you to come to the funeral. I think it went rather well, don't you?"

"Ah, yeah, great funeral," I said.

"Is Graham home? I thought we might play if he is."

I opened the door wider to admit him entry. "Sure, Conner. He's upstairs."

"You looked quite lovely in that gray dress you wore today, Mrs. Pugh."

I sighed. "Thank you, Conner," I said.

"I'll just go upstairs now," he said, and matched the action to the words.

I stood watching the littlest McLemore as he jovially bounced his way through my kitchen into the dining room. He still reminded me of someone I'd seen on TV, but it was no longer Eddie Haskell. The late-night vision of Patty McCormack in *The Bad Seed* sprang to mind.

No, I told myself, shaking my head. He's too little. No way he could have strangled Brad. Unless Mom or Dad helped.

I shuddered at the thought and went outside to begin my spring yard work.

Roy Lester had been an avid gardener, as were most of the people on our street. Only one house in the neighborhood sprouted eternal weeds, and that house belonged to the Pughs. We are not what you'd call fastidious when it comes to the yards, front or back. Willis's tools were all neatly hung up on pegs in the garage. I even had a separate drawer exclusively for lids to my Tupperware. But when it came to the yards and the implements employed upon them, we were known to be a trifle lazy. We tried to remember to pick up rakes and the like, especially after Willis stepped on one and the handle sprang up and hit him between the eyes, almost knocking him out. It was very funny, of course, to watch, but Willis had missed the humor.

That was why there was no need for me to go into the garage hunting for the soaker hose to use on the new plants I'd planted in the border by the front door. The hoses remained year in and year out attached to the spigots in the yards. I pulled the hose out from behind a bush where it had been haphazardly tossed and began stretching it across the border with the new azalea bushes—my fourth attempt at azaleas. These would die before they ever bloomed, just like all the others, but if one had no hope, one had nothing.

I'm not sure which of my senses picked it up first, sight or touch, though I'm betting heavily on touch. I really think it was the feel of the flat, one-inch wide strip of plastic hose with the quarter-inch ridges next to the holes for the soaker that made me look at it in the first place. If I'd been in a movie, they would have superimposed the image of Brad McLemore's bruised neck right over the thing in my hands.

I dropped it as if it were covered in blood.

Six

I was in the kitchen with Luna while Willis was in the front yard watching a uniformed officer dust the hose for fingerprints.

"I doubt there will be any prints," Luna said, "unless the perp has never watched TV in his life."

"I touched it," I said from the kitchen sink where I was doing a Tony-award winning imitation of Lady Macbeth.

"We'll have to take your prints and Willis's so we'll know if we have an extra set."

"I touched it,' I repeated.

Luna stood up and walked to the sink and turned the water off, leaving me with soap-covered hands. "You're losing it, Pugh."

"May I rinse my hands, please?"

She turned the water on, keeping the faucet on to measure out only enough water to actually rinse the soap off. Then she turned it off, gave me a kitchen towel, and walked me to the table. I kept the towel with me as I sat, hands under the table, surreptitiously rubbing them raw with the terry cloth.

I contemplated the fact that there's only so much the human mind can take before it snaps. With what someone less graciously inclined might consider self-pity, I figured I'd had more than enough to do the trick. Forget about what I'd gone through less than a year before with my best friends and neighbors; forget about taking a new child into my family. Forget all that. Just consider the 911 calls, the glass in the chocolate, the destruction of my front door, the rummaging of my jewelry, the filth on my computer, the ads in the papers, the stolen check, the sex toys, Brad McLemore staring at my house all hours of the night, his dead body found in my car, and now having actually touched the murder weapon. My hands actually touched the thing that was pulled around Brad's neck hard enough and long enough to choke the life from his body.

Without a word to Luna, I got up and walked out of the kitchen, through the dining room, the living room, to the foyer and up the stairs. I didn't realize Luna had followed me until she took the suitcase I'd just pulled down from the top shelf of my bedroom closet out of my hand.

"What's this for?" she asked.

"I'm leaving. Just one suitcase for me. I can get the girls' stuff into one, and a duffel bag for Graham. Will you take the cats? Or Willis can if he refuses to leave. He probably will. He thinks his work is so important. Ha! I guess I should call my mother—let her get ready for us—"

"You can't go anywhere, Pugh," Luna said. Under other circumstances I might have noticed that her voice was gentler than usual.

I roughly pulled the suitcase out of her hands. "Hide and watch!" I said, throwing the case on the bed, opening it, and tossing underwear in from the bureau drawers. Luna was tossing the clothing back in as fast as I was taking it out. "Stop that!" I finally said, hitting her hand.

She pushed me to a sitting position on the bed. "You stop it, Pugh. Pull yourself together."

"Thank you, but no. I prefer hysteria. It's less taxing."

"You can handle this."

"I don't want to."

"You have to."

"Not if I don't want to."

Luna sighed and sank down on the bed next to me, pushing the mostly empty suitcase out of her way. "You can't run away from this, E.J. I know after all you've been through, all your kids have been through, that that's what you want to do, but you can't. For one thing, it's the coward's way out, and you're not a coward. Secondly—"

She stopped and looked longingly at the light fixture on the ceiling. It was nothing special, just your run of the mill, standard-issue, housing development, master bedroom light fixture. "Secondly what?" I demanded.

Luna sighed. "The powers that be at the Codderville PD think you're the most likely suspect. So you can't leave town."

I started laughing. I'm not sure when I quit.

Luna left me lying on the bed. I'd given her instructions to tell Willis that the children were his responsibility for as long as I cared to stay sequestered in my room. My thought at the moment was I might get up to see them each graduate high school.

I had things to think about. Major things. Like Luna was right to stare at the light fixture. It was quite attractive. And what about that stain on the ceiling? Was that a water stain? Huh? Did we have a leak? And wasn't it interesting that the stain looked like a standard Rorschach test; but if I turned my head slightly to the left it took on the shape of a bunny rabbit and, slightly to the right, it looked like someone shooting the finger.

All this was my way of not thinking about the one thing I really needed to be thinking about: namely, if Brad McLemore had been doing all those horrible things to me, if he had been my stalker, then who had been his? Because Brad was definitely dead, and not by his own hands. And also not by mine. Someone had killed that sad, pathetic boy. Why? Was he not alone in his harassing of me? But Brad had no friends. He was never with another boy. Always alone. Unless it was a member of his weirder-than-weird family, he had to be acting alone. So then, who killed him? A would-be burglar? A passing serial killer?

I rolled over on my side to get away from staring at the bunny rabbit/finger. Like the verbal finger Brad McLemore had given me when I accused him of harassing me. *Who'd want to look at a fat old cow like you?* he'd said. Serious denial? Or had he really been after another member of my family? One of the children, or even Willis? Of course, if it had been me, what else would he have said? *Yes, my darling. I can't deny my lust for you any longer!*

I rolled onto the other side and decided maybe I'd been writing romances a little too long.

Luna had been right about one thing: I wasn't a coward. But I'd been acting like one. I'd been hiding in my house while someone outside was banging on the door. I needed to do something with the fear and the anger. The best thing for me was action. I wasn't my mother; scrubbing the kitchen floor in times of emergency wasn't my style. Mindless busywork wasn't going to stop the harassment, harassment that someone had ended in Brad McLemore's murder.

I made a phone call, left the kids with Willis, and headed into Codderville.

Anne Comstock is a therapist with a lot of letters after her name, which all boil down to the fact that she's a licensed practitioner in the State of Texas and a practicing psychotherapist in Codderville. She's the one the whole family had gone to after the Lester family had been murdered last year. She was the one we were seeing now to get ready for Bessie's legal adoption into the family, the day she would legally become Elizabeth Lester Pugh. Anne had agreed to meet me at her office, due to the emergency nature of the situation, which I'd briefly told her about on the phone.

I read, I watch TV, I know all about psychological profiles. I parked in the parking lot of Anne's building, feeling only slightly guilty about the fact that Anne thought she was rushing to her office to help me deal with the fear and anger the situation had caused, not to help me solve the problem.

Anne met me at the door of her office, decked out in running shorts and a T-shirt, the most casual I'd ever seen her. "E.J., hi! Come on in." She put her arm across my shoulders and ushered me into her office. "I just started the coffeepot. It should be ready in a minute."

"Sounds great."

We sat in our usual seats: Anne in the desk chair, facing me in the more comfortable easy chair.

"So, tell me," she said. "What's been going on?"

I told her in detail all of the things that had been happening.

"Anne, what I really need from you is help in trying to figure out who's doing this. Do you know anything about psychological profiling?"

Anne smiled. "It's not my specialty, E.J. But I've read some books and articles on the subject."

I settled back in my chair. "Anything you can give me would help, Anne. At this point I'm feeling my way in the dark."

Anne considered a moment, then said, "I think there are two different people at work here, E.J. Brad and someone else. From what you said, Brad was a voyeur—a Peeping Tom. In my dealings with voyeurs, I've noticed one thing that stands out about them: they don't want to get caught. They're in this for the thrill of frightening someone. They make obscene phone calls, peek in windows. And they touch the things that belong to others."

The voyeurs she'd dealt with? This was a small community. I wanted to ask "Who? Who?" but knew I couldn't. Briefly I wondered if it was Mr. Hinkly at the drugstore. I saw him looking at my butt one day in the reflection of the plate glass window. Or could it be Stew Griffith at the Texaco? He was *very* friendly.

"I think it's safe to assume," Anne said (while I tried to get back on track), "that Brad's the one who went through your jewelry. He probably went through your underwear drawer, too."

I shuddered and Anne touched me lightly on the arm. "It would fit the pattern. I'm sorry. Go home and soak the entire contents of the drawer in Woolite for a day or two. It'll make you feel better." She smiled. "Anyway, voyeurs don't usually stalk. They don't usually do harm. Although, and this is going to sound contradictory, a lot of stalkers and rapists were once voyeurs. It just doesn't fit that all voyeurs will become stalkers and rapists. Do you follow me?"

I nodded my head.

"This other person—more than likely the one who killed Brad—is different. What do you think he wants?"

I shook my head. "He's never said. The one phone call I got was so quick. I hung up the phone as soon as I realized who it was. . . . Maybe I shouldn't have done that?"

"It's human nature to disconnect from something that frightening as quickly as possible. But it doesn't fit the profile I've read about. They usually start with demands, and when their victim doesn't meet their demands, the harassment escalates." She stopped for a moment, staring off into space. Finally she said, "I don't want to frighten you, E.J."

"I don't think it could get much worse, Anne. Let me have it."

Anne sighed. "The personal ad I think is very telling, along with the sex toys and the crap on the computer—"

"The computer had to be Brad. He was there at the house—"

Anne shook her head, frowning. "It doesn't fit. Too aggressive for his style. Is there any other way? Anybody else in the house? Some outside source—"

I hit my head like I coulda had a V8. "Jesus! The modem!"

Anne leaned forward. "Tell me about it."

"I'm hooked up directly to Willis's office. But a computer hacker could get in through the modem, I suppose. I wouldn't know how, but I think they could."

"Who at Willis's office would have access to his computer?"

"His secretary Angel, she sends me things all the time by modem. This guy he's thinking of taking on as a partner, Doug. Willis has two part-time drafters, one female, one male—but neither one of them has been around for months. And I've never even met the male. And clients." I leaned my head back. "Well, this is narrowing it down."

The sarcasm wasn't lost on Anne. She smiled. "It *is* narrowing it down, E.J. We've narrowed it down to someone with access to and a knowledge of computers."

"I interrupted you. You were on a roll about the sex toys and the stuff on the computer—"

"Right. The ad. That's what bothers me. The well-endowed part."

I looked at my chest. "Well, I am."

Anne grinned, looking at her own slightly flat chest. "There are those who say small-breasted women are more intelligent."

"But we know how stupid they are, don't we?" I said, grinning back.

Anne laughed. "One of these days we're going to have lunch and discuss that, but," she sobered, "as of now, I think he's telling you something."

"What?"

"Well, I hate to get Freudian, but saying you were well-endowed in the ad, sending you sex toys, writing the pornography on the computer, I would hazard a guess the guy thinks you're loose. He's set you up as impure for some reason. Maybe it's a hang-up about his mother—" She held up her hand to ward off my skepticism. "Clichés become clichés because they're truths that happen too often. Okay, what does he know about you? He knows you're a mother. He knows what you look like. He's obviously attracted to your body, but it also frightens him, offends him. Makes him angry."

I sighed. "This is all great stuff, Anne. But what does he look like? How old is he? Where does he live? What's his name?"

Anne smiled and shook her head. "Sorry. I'm only a shrink. No crystal balls here." She leaned forward in her chair. "But, E.J., there are some needs I want to talk about."

I nodded my head.

"I need to make sure you're protecting yourself

and the kids. That you're taking the proper precautions. Have you asked the police about protection?"

"Not really—"

"Ask. That's why we pay taxes. My other need is this: to help you deal with your emotions right now. I understand that you're angry and that you're frightened. I want you to articulate those fears. Tell me what they are." She held up her hand and started counting her fingers. "One, two, three." She put her hand down. "Your number-one fear?"

"That he'll hurt the children."

She nodded her head. "What are you doing and what can you do to see this doesn't happen?"

"I'm not letting them go outside much to play. I take them to school and pick them up." I shook my head. "I've thought about sending them to Houston to stay with my parents, but I don't know—"

"What are your concerns about sending them to Houston?"

I sighed. "I wouldn't be with them. I wouldn't know for sure that they're okay every second of every day. I wouldn't know when they could come home." I stood up and began to pace the worn carpet in Anne's office. "And he'd win, damnit! He'd be taking the most precious part of my life away from me. My kids! And I'd be helping him do it!"

"Do you think you and Willis can keep them safe?"

I sat back down. "I don't know."

"What's your second fear?"

"That he'll kill me or maim me. That my kids will grow up without a mom, or with a mom who can't function properly." I tried a grin. "And if he kills me, Willis would have carte blanche to start dating again. We can't have that."

"What's fear number three?"

I thought for a moment. And I wondered if this really wasn't right up there with fears number one and two. "That this will go on forever. That he'll never show himself but just keep this up. That there will be no resolution."

"So you're putting on your Nancy Drew hat and you're going to solve this yourself?" Anne said, smiling that therapist smile.

"I can't just sit back. Not my style."

"Don't you trust the police?"

I thought about that for a moment. "It's not that I don't trust them. They're just not personally involved. They don't have as much at stake in this as I do."

Anne stood, indicating the time was up. Personally, I could have gone on for hours, hashing and rehashing, but then I would have had to take out a government loan to pay for the time. She walked me to the door and I headed home, not knowing how ironic that last question was going to turn out to be.

I had another thought as I left Anne's office. One thing I hadn't done was find out, really find out, about Brad McLemore. I had my impression of him, his mother's impression of him, but all that was from a slanted, adult perspective. What I needed was a peer analysis.

Monique Lester had been my ticket into the world of the teenager. After her death the year before, I'd not kept up much with her friends. Her best friend, Wendy Beck, had baby-sat for us for a while, until she got a car and an afterschool job and had no more need for the pittance we could pay her. She worked at one of the stores in the Codderville mini-mall out on the highway. I drove there, parked, and went in to find her. I couldn't remember which store, knowing only that it was a women's dress shop. I found her in the third store I looked in.

Wendy and Monique had been best friends since first grade. Monique's death had hit Wendy hard—

harder than the other kids in school, a lot of whom had been close to Monique. Monique had been pretty special, and a lot of people had picked up on that. She had been popular. Wendy was that peculiar phenomenon: the not-so-attractive, not-very-popular girl who was the closest ally of the queen bee. All queen bees have them; some just hide them away and use them for the serious, heart-wrenching discussions, the giggles about the things that *really* matter.

Monique hadn't treated her lady-in-waiting like that. Where you found Monique, you found Wendy. If a boy asked out Monique, he better have a friend willing to go out with Wendy. If Monique was invited to a party, it was common knowledge that Wendy was, too. For months after Monique's death, the few times I saw Wendy when she'd baby-sat for us, I had seen the young girl wither. When I'd been around the two of them, they were both active, excited, ready to break out. Wendy was the one who could always bring Monique out of a mood, make her laugh. She was a funny girl. The humor had been missing when she baby-sat. Bessie, Monique's little sister, was the only person Wendy was able to shine around. She'd gained weight, too, the puffy, I'm-eating-because-I'm-miserable kind of weight. I hadn't seen her in five months.

The girl I found at Brendle's Boutique was not the girl I'd last seen. The boutique handled the kind of clothes only someone with a lot of self-esteem could handle. Those were the clothes Wendy was wearing: a tight, short mini-skirt of dark leather over a tight-fitting bodysuit. And she looked great. She'd lost the miserable pounds, and her shiny hair was long down her back. When she saw me, she smiled and ran to me, hugging me.

"God, Miz Pugh! It's great to see you!"

I smiled. "You look fantastic!" I said. "Tell me your secret!"

She grinned. "Hey, I'm in love. What can I say?"

Well, that certainly explained that. I asked her if she could take a break. She checked with her supervisor, got the okay, and we went out into the mall to the food court. She grabbed a slice of pizza and a Coke while I found a cup of semi-decent coffee.

"Tell me all about him," I said, grinning at her.

"His name's Daniel and he just moved to the school this semester." She sobered. "He didn't know Monique. I'm in counseling now with Anne Comstock—"

"She's Bessie's counselor—"

"Yeah, I know. Well, it's like with everybody else, I was just an extension of Monique. And when she died, it was like I didn't have any reason to be around, you know?" I nodded my head. "Nobody invited me to parties, or even talked to me, really." She sighed. "I can't really blame them. I wasn't a lot of fun after she died." She shrugged. "Maybe I wasn't much before she died—with anybody but her, you know?"

I reached out and touched her hand. "I'm sorry—"

She squeezed my hand, then went back to her pizza. "I miss her. I'll always miss her, but maybe I needed to be away from her. I needed to find out I was my own person." She stopped. "Oh, God, that sounds so awful, you know? But that's not what I meant—"

I smiled. "I know what you meant, Wendy. It's kind of hard to see the stars when the sun's shining."

Wendy leaned back in her seat and looked at me. "God, that's good." She grabbed her purse and pulled out a small spiral notebook. "Can I write that down?"

I laughed. "Sure," I said.

"I'm writing now," she said, grinning. "Just like you. I got a short story published in the school magazine, and one of my teachers sent it to a teen mag, and they're considering it. So, you know, I'd, like, *use* that line?"

I shrugged. "It's yours."

She grinned. "Cool."

She put away the notebook and took the last bite of her pizza. "So, what brings you out here, anyway?" she asked.

"Well, I wanted to ask you about Brad McLemore. Did you know him?"

She winced. "Gross, huh? I mean, it's like that house is cursed or something, you know? I heard it was your hose that did it, right?"

"Where'd you hear that?" I asked, wondering how that information got out so fast.

"Daniel's mom is the dispatcher at the police station. He knows *everything*," she said proudly.

"Yeah, it was my hose," I said, suppressing a shudder.

"Jeez, gross."

"Did you know Brad?"

She shrugged. "Not to really talk to, you know? He was a real geek. Didn't have any friends at all that I ever knew about. I guess I shouldn't talk like that. Six months ago I was a female version of Brad McLemore."

"Never," I said, smiling. "Did he have any teachers he was close to, anything like that?"

Wendy shook her head. "No. I had one class with him this semester, but he sat in the back of the room—when he came. I don't think he showed up much."

"Did he ever participate in class?"

Again Wendy shook her head. "I'm telling you, Miz Pugh. The guy was a zero. He just wasn't *there*, ya know?"

I nodded my head. I knew. "Nobody you can think of I can talk to about him?"

Wendy shook her head. "I wish I could help you,

but, God, you know, like, I just can't think of *any-body*." Her face lit up. "But I'll ask around and give you a call, okay?"

"Great," I said. "I'd really appreciate it."

We talked a little more—about her parents, her brothers, some of the other kids in Monique's circle that I'd known. I told her about Bessie, about how well she was doing. About the need for the cussing jar. She laughed. I left the mall missing Monique more than I had in months.

We didn't get in to the Codderville PD to have our fingerprints taken until four-thirty Monday afternoon. As much as I knew Graham would have enjoyed seeing his parents fingerprinted, I thought it the better part of valor to find a baby-sitter. The only baby-sitter I had left since Monique's death was my mother-in-law Vera, who had a standing four P.M. Monday hair appointment and had had since 1952. The only time she'd canceled had been due to the birth of Willis's brother Rusty. I didn't figure having her daughter-in-law being fingerprinted as a murder suspect was enough justification for another cancellation.

The station wagon was still impounded, so Willis had to come home to get me. He brought Angel with him. Gracious lady that she was, she'd accepted the challenge but declined the triple-time pay Willis had offered her to baby-sit.

As we drove off he told me of her refusal. "Don't worry," I said. "She'll accept it by the time we come back. Maybe even ask for more after an hour or two with Graham and company."

There's a reason why we don't have a long list of eager teenagers ready to make an easy buck off the Pughs. There's nothing easy about a buck made at our house.

It only took about twenty minutes to fingerprint

both Willis and me. The extra hour was taken up by Police Chief Catfish Watkins's interrogation of his prime suspect.

"The boy'd been bothering you some, huh, Miz Pugh?"

"He had been observed staring into our windows late at night."

"Observed by who?"

"Me."

"You the only one seen him peeping?"

"Yes."

"So you got no corroborating evidence to support your accusation?"

"No."

"Detective Luna tells me you even accused this boy of rifling through your jewelry, that true?"

"Yes."

"When would he a-done this, Miz Pugh?"

"I'm not sure of the date, although I'm sure the Codderville Memorial emergency room records could tell you. It was the day my daughter was taken to the emergency room for ingesting candy laced with glass." I tried to lighten my voice. It was getting tighter and tighter—as tight as my grip on Willis's hand.

"Why was the boy in your home?"

"Because I needed someone to stay with my other children while I went with Megan in the ambulance."

"I sure hope your little girl's okay?"

"She's fine, thank you."

"Now, according to Detective Luna's records, you got some other stuff going on here, Miz Pugh. Like, nasty stuff written on your computer and dirty underwear or something coming in the mail?"

"Yes."

"You think the boy did this?"

"I don't really know. He could have been working with someone else. I just don't know."

"Uh-huh," Catfish said, his drawl nice and easy. Like the gentle clang of a cell door closing. "Seems to me this boy's been messing with your head pretty bad, Miz Pugh. Lots a people'd be real upset, what with all that going on."

I remained silent.

"Seems to me a lot of people'd be so upset they'd want to do something to stop his shenanigans. You know, like have a talk with the boy if they saw him in the yard or something. Sometimes a little talking to like that can escalate, Miz Pugh. Maybe end up in a fist fight. A slap in the face."

"If I killed him, Chief, do you think I'd be stupid enough to put his body in my own car?"

"Well, now, Miz Pugh, if you was stupid enough to kill him—"

Willis, who'd requested to sit in on the interrogation with me, stood up. I wasn't sure how well Catfish Watkins knew my husband, although he had been a friend of Willis's father for years. I wasn't sure if Catfish knew him well enough to recognize the set of the shoulders, the slight tick on the left side of his mouth, or the glint in his eye. I'd only seen the symptoms once before—right before he body-slammed a mugger on the streets of Houston.

"That's enough, Chief," Willis said between clinched teeth. "If you wish to talk with my wife again, it will be with our lawyer."

Catfish laughed. A jovial, good-ol'-boy laugh. "Now, Willis, your wife ain't being charged with nothing here. We're just chewing the fat, so to speak."

"That's fine, Catfish. Meanwhile, it's late and we need to get home and feed the kids."

I stood up next to Willis and took the hand the chief held out to me. He shook it formally. "Hope I didn't offend you, Miz Pugh. Just trying to figure out what's going on here."

"Uh-hum," I said, and led the way out the door of the chief's office.

"I didn't kill Brad McLemore," I said, staring straight ahead of me in the car, looking at the early evening sun setting to the west as we drove northwest home.

"I know," Willis said.

I looked at my husband. God, he'd been the most gorgeous guy at U.T. in 1973. Like Robert Redford with height and an attitude. I'd seen him around campus, seen him at the hangouts on the drag across from the main gate. My roommate Marie and I had plotted ways for me to meet him, but I'd always chickened out. It had been pure serendipity that I'd worn those particular shoes to class that day. They were new and the soles were slick. Marie and I had met outside my class and were taking the stairs down to the front door of the chem building. The uncarpeted stairs were as slick as the soles of my shoes. When the two met they took an immediate dislike to each other, throwing me up in the air. I landed on my bottom and butt-scooted down half a flight of stairs to the landing. It was so comical a sight that Marie had fallen against the wall laughing. Everyone on the staircase that day was laughing. I came to an abrupt halt on the landing, my books and papers scattered around me, my jeans ripped, one shoe broken, and my pride two points below zero.

He had come out of nowhere—the only person not laughing. He'd knelt beside me, asking if I was okay. I feigned pain, although there was none—no physical pain, that is. He helped me gently to my feet and knelt to retrieve my books and papers. Then he said he bet after all that I could use a beer. I agreed. We've rarely been apart since that moment.

I trusted Willis with my life and my love. He'd never given me reason to doubt that trust. I'd sometimes wondered how much domestic bliss—Pugh-style—he could handle, but he'd been a real trooper through all the hell we'd been through in our lives together. Was this to be another test? Having your wife suspected of a crime as brutal as murdering a teenaged boy? If Catfish Watkins pursued his suspicions against me, how long would it take for Willis to wonder if maybe, just maybe, I *had* done something? If the shoe was on the other foot, how long would it take me? How loyal would I be? How forgiving and trusting?

I wanted to think the answer was forever, totally, absolutely. That I would stand by my man better than Tammy Wynette could ever sing about. But suspicion is an insidious, subtle thing. When all around you are pointing fingers, whispering, saying, "There she goes. She's the one who—" How long before that little worm of doubt would creep into his brain, making a beeline for his heart?

I touched Willis's hand where it rested on the steering wheel. He took my hand in his hand and put it to his mouth, kissing it lightly. I was scared. Terrified. Not only could I lose my freedom, I could lose Willis. I could lose my life.

The kids had been fed and bathed and were in their nightclothes when we got back to the house. The girls were sitting on either side of Angel, and Graham sat at her feet while she read from *The Cat in the Hat*. The TV was off and the cats were all three in Angel's lap.

"Pay her an extra month's salary," I suggested to Willis as we took in the scene of domestic tranquility.

"I was thinking a year's," he said.

Seven

Things got back to relatively normal after a while. I didn't hear anything from Catfish or Luna, giving me what I hoped wasn't a false sense of security. The car was released from being impounded, so I was able to resume my life of motherly and wifely chores. The first time I got in the car it was difficult to even look at the backseat. Instead of buckling the kids in I let them ride loose in the cargo area in the rear of the wagon. I knew I couldn't do this indefinitely. I would either have to sell the car or get used to my children sitting on the spot where Brad McLemore's dead body had lain. Since we couldn't afford a new car, or even a used one, I was going to have to deal with the alternative.

I tried to keep my mind sane and empty as I took Willis's shirts to the laundry (I don't iron and Willis doesn't like permanent press; we compromise), baked three dozen cupcakes for Megan's class, made a sword out of cardboard and tinfoil for Graham's class's production of *Peter Pan*, took Ernie to the vet for seizure medication, patched up Axl Rose's left ear from a cat fight, called the plumber to repair the leaky upstairs toilet that Willis had taken apart and couldn't get back together, cooked more meals than one would consider healthy, washed more laundry than one would consider possible, and managed to churn out three chapters of *Reflections in Turquoise*. (Yes, Branson and Lavana finally did it. We're all so proud.)

My major difficulty during that time seemed to be in having the back of my office chair facing into the kitchen. When the refrigerator motor would whirr to life, I'd jump up and run into the kitchen, brandishing a kitchen knife. I only left one window open in the house; even though the early April weather was something I'd usually enjoy, when I'd open all the windows to let the winter-dead air out of the house. But even that one opened window had me whirling around in my seat every time a bird chirped or a neighbor slammed a car door. I finally had Willis help me rearrange my little office so that my back was no longer to the door. My paranoia didn't lessen; it was just easier to keep an eye on the empty kitchen and open window.

I managed in that week and a half of domestic bliss to stay as far away from Ginger McLemore as possible. At the end of that time, however, was the Spring Fling at the elementary school. With three kids in three different classes at the same school, it would have been difficult not to participate. The finale of the Spring Fling was the fourth-grade's mini-production of *Peter Pan*, in which Graham had a minor role as one of the Lost Boys. I had been roped (no pun intended) into working the curtain for the production. I'd also been persuaded to man the fishing booth for Bessie's kindergarten class and make three dozen *cascarones* (eggshells filled with confetti) for Megan's class. These the kids bought for a quarter, then bashed against the heads of every adult they could find. It's always great fun.

I got to the school early with Graham. Willis was to come an hour later with the girls. Graham ran to the "cafetorium" (for those of you blessed with no school-aged offspring, this is a generic school term for a combination cafeteria/auditorium) to join his class for last-minute preparations for the show, and I took my *cascarones* to Megan's teacher's room, as I'd been instructed. After dropping off the eggshells, I hightailed it across the hall to Bessie's teacher's room to find out where I was supposed to set up my fishing booth.

The materials were all there: a large cardboard stand, painted blue and white to look like water, with holes cut into it; plastic "fishing poles"; and all the prizes. The object of the fishing booth is this: A kid rents a fishing pole for a quarter, I help him or her stick it through the hole in the backdrop, then I run around behind it and stick a prize on the end of the pole and the kid pulls it through the hole and is disappointed that all he got for his quarter was some stupid Batman stickers. Or a plastic spinning top. Or a plastic replica of a Ninja Turtle. Or something else of equal or lesser (preferably lesser) value.

I was on the sidewalk leading to the kindergarten classes setting up my booth when Ginger McLemore approached me. As she was president of the Black Cat Ridge Elementary PTA, I wasn't all that surprised to see her. She was sort of the head honcho in charge of everything for the Spring Fling.

"E.J.," she sang out, smiling her always present smile.

I stopped what I was doing (setting aside the prizes I wanted my own kids to get) and waited for her to walk up to me. "Hi, Ginger."

She never stopped smiling. "Did you kill Brad?" she asked.

I was stunned. Shocked. Scared. "What? Ginger, how could you think—"

"Catfish Watkins told Arthur you're his prime suspect." The smile never left the perfect oval of her face. "Did you do it?"

"Of course not, Ginger, how could you ask—"

She slapped me. The impact was so hard and so unexpected I almost lost my balance. Kids were beginning to show up for the Spring Fling, so there were more than a dozen or so pint-sized witnesses and even some parents.

Arthur McLemore took that minute to show up. He put his hands on his wife's shoulders and pulled her gently away from me. "Hi, E.J.," he said. "How you doing?"

Why was it every time I was around these people I had the feeling I'd stepped through Alice's looking glass? "Fine, Arthur," I said, rubbing the stinging place on my cheek from Ginger's slap. "How are you?"

"Oh, we're doing just great. Come on, honey," he said to Ginger. "The principal's looking for you. Say 'bye to E.J."

" 'Bye, E.J.," Ginger said, giving me a little wave with her fingers.

As I watched them walk away, my first sucker showed up with a quarter in his grubby, cotton candy-sticky hand. I rewarded him with a spider ring in a clear plastic bubble and sent him disappointedly on his way, wondering if Ginger would ever be able to understand if I said to her, "Thanks, I needed that." Because that slap in the face was just the thing I *did* need. The fear that had been sitting in the bottom of my stomach ready to spew forth at any moment was finally gone. I was no longer afraid. I was pissed. Seriously, totally, undeniably pissed.

"And then she slapped me," I said. We were spooning to the left that night: Willis's arm draped across my waist, his knees tucked into the curve of my knees, his breath ruffling my hair.

"What did you do?"

"What could I do? Nothing. Arthur showed up and led her away." I took a deep breath. "She smiled and waved bye-bye. Actually waved bye-bye, like a little kid."

"Drugs, you think?" my husband, the great experimenter of the seventies, asked.

I shrugged, which unfortunately hit Willis in the chin and made him bite his tongue. We dealt with that for a moment and reversed spoons. "All I know is that she's the weirdest woman on God's green earth, Willis. She is certifiable. Which is the only explanation for her volunteering to be PTA president in the first place. We should have seen this coming."

"I can't believe she slapped you," Willis said.

"Think about how I felt! I was the slapee! And everybody and their brother standing around staring! It was awful."

"They're weird. Both of them. Oh, I forgot to tell you," Willis said, rising up and upsetting the spoon. I lay on my back and looked up at him as he leaned over me. "Arthur stopped me yesterday when I pulled in the driveway. Guess what he wanted?"

"God only knows."

"To show me his new putter. I swear to God. His kid buried less than a month and he's out buying new golf clubs. And, jeez, he was excited. Personally, I don't think it's normal for a grown man to get excited about a new golf club."

"New software, however, is perfectly understandable," I teased.

"Software is totally different. That's important."

"To you."

He lay back down, rolling me over for a spoon to the left, but by this time the covers were totally disheveled and it took another few minutes to straighten them out before we settled down again. "All I know," I said, "is that I'm not crazy about living next door to the Stepford family."

Willis rolled away from me. "Where'd you go?" I asked.

"I'm not going to discuss moving. I'm not."

I sighed. I'd been thinking of a condo in Vail.

It was ten A.M. the following Tuesday. I was well into the part of the book where Lavana realizes she's in love with Branson and that Branson might have a thing for her, too, especially after one whole chapter of uninterrupted nookie. This meant I was only a few chapters away from wrapping up the whole unseemly mess, when the phone rang.

I left the computer and went into the kitchen to pick up the phone. "Hello?" I said.

"Mommy! Mommy, help! Mommy! Help me! Help me!"

"Megan? Bessie? Is that you? What's going on? Honey, where are you?"

"Mommy! Mommy!" Then I heard the most blood-curdling scream I've ever heard. Right before the line went dead in my hands.

I grabbed the cordless phone and my keys and ran out of the house, leaving the door open in my haste to get to the car. I dialed Luna's number as I started the car and pulled out of the driveway. I had about half a block before the cordless would go dead. I prayed that Luna would answer and answer quickly. She did.

"One of my girls is in trouble! I'm headed for the

school. I got a call with her screaming help. Luna—"
My voice broke as my foot hit the accelerator.

"I'm on my—" That's all I heard as the phone
went out of range. I threw it on the seat and broke
every traffic law in the state of Texas as I raced the
five blocks to the Black Cat Ridge Elementary. I ran
the station wagon halfway onto the sidewalk and left
it there, the motor running, as I ran inside the school,
racing down the halls toward the kindergarten
rooms. I flung open the first door, the door to Bessie's
room, just as the assistant principal caught up with
me, obviously having seen my panicked arrival at
the school. Bessie was sitting at a table doing finger-
paints. Her face lit up when she saw me, but I just
turned, shoving the assistant principal out of the way
as I rushed across the hall to Megan's room and flung
that door open. They were in the middle of story
time. Megan was braiding a girl's hair who sat next
to her.

They were okay. They were both okay. Graham.
Could it have been Graham's voice? Pitched high in
panic? The assistant principal, Miss Reading, grabbed
my arm. "Mrs. Pugh, what *are* you doing?"

"Graham!" I yelled and started running down the
hall, out of that wing and onto the main wing of the
school where the fourth-grade classes were.

"Mrs. Pugh, now you just stop this right now!" I
heard Miss Reading say, the tap-tap of her leather-
soled shoes fast behind me.

I got to Graham's door and flung it open. He was
sitting in his usual seat. He looked at me, rolled his
eyes, and turned red. Nothing like having your crazy
mother burst in to embarrass you in front of your
buds.

I slammed the door and leaned up against the wall,
panting for breath. Miss Reading caught up with me,
followed close behind by Luna.

"E.J.?" Luna yelled, running up.

"They're okay," I said. "All three are okay."

Luna fell up against the wall beside me, panting as hard as I was.

Miss Reading, a prissy little thing two years out of college, pursed her lips and frowned. "Would you mind telling me what the devil is going on here?"

"Not particularly," Luna said, taking my arm and leading me out of the school. We sat down on the curb in front of my station wagon, both still breathing like marathon runners.

"Tell me," Luna said.

I shook my head. "I guess the line wasn't terribly clear. I couldn't even tell if it was Bessie's or Megan's voice. Just a little-girl voice screaming 'Mommy.'" I shuddered. "It was the most horrible thing I've ever heard."

Luna sighed and patted my knee. "There's always the chance this was some little-girl-lost dialing the wrong number. If that's true, we'll have a report of a child missing before evening." She turned and looked at me. "But I don't think that's going to happen, E.J. I don't think this was a wrong number. But what scares me is that Brad McLemore's dead. We can't blame this on him."

I realized I'd just begun to get pissed off about the slap on the face by Ginger McLemore. Using my children's safety to harass me was more than I could stomach. All of the other things—with the exception of the glass-laced candy—had been aimed at me, had been really nothing more than nuisance and embarrassment. But now he—she—it—was using my children. And now I was as angry as I'd ever been.

I left Luna sitting on the curb and drove into Codderville to Willis's office. Angel greeted me as I came in the door.

"Hey, E.J.! How you doing?"

I tried a smile, although it felt foreign to the muscles of my mouth. "Fine, Angel, how are you?"

"Oh, fine. If you're looking for Willis, he's out of the office right—"

"But who needs Willis when I'm here?" Doug Kingsley said from the doorway of the big room.

I turned toward Doug. "Do you know where I can reach him?"

Doug frowned and moved toward me. "E.J., is something wrong?"

I hugged my arms to my sides and shook my head. I was trying very hard to keep my anger, my fears, my emotions in check. I obviously wasn't doing a really good job of it. "I just need to talk with him," I said.

Doug moved closer and put his arm around me, leading me toward the door of Willis's private office. "That son-of-a-bitch police chief hasn't been giving you any shit again, has he?"

Doug sat me down on the loveseat in Willis's office, closing the door behind him, and he sat down next to me with his arm back around my shoulders. "Willis is out on a bid on that Chemco job. He should be back in an hour or so." He put his finger under my chin and lifted my face to his. "But you don't look like you can wait an hour."

I pulled slightly away. My attraction to Doug Kingsley was fast waning. I'm not fond of being touched by people I don't know well. And in my present mood, a little extramarital touchy-feely just wasn't what I was looking for. One of the things I like best about Luna is that, even after all we'd gone through a year before, Luna had never tried to hug me. You gotta like that in a woman.

I stood up and moved to the door. "As soon as Willis gets back have him call me, okay?" And I was out of there like a shot.

I drove home, pulling into the driveway. My front

door stood wide open, just like I left it. Unfortunately, the living room wasn't like I'd left it. My furniture was rearranged. The couch was upside down blocking the fireplace, and the matching loveseat and easy chair were upside down in a vaguely mating position. The coffee tables and end tables were on the stairs. The chairs in the dining room were stacked one on top of the other, reaching the ceiling. On the top chair, arranged in such a way that it appeared a very flat human was sitting there, were a pair of oversize twill shorts, a Nirvana T-shirt, and Brad McLemore's dirty tennis shoes.

Luna put down the portable phone and looked at me. "The chief wants to know how come Brad McLemore's clothes, if they are his clothes, are in your house."

"They're his clothes, all right," I said, sinking down in an easy chair after uprighting it. "His style, anyway. And I'd swear the shoes are his. I'd never seen him in another pair."

"E.J., this doesn't look good."

I rolled my eyes. "How stupid, how incredibly stupid does Catfish Watkins think I am, Luna? Or maybe I'm just nuts, is that it?"

"You went through a terrible strain last year," Luna said quietly.

I got up from the chair and moved to the front door. "If you're through, Detective, I suggest you leave my house."

"E.J., I'm just trying to tell you how this looks to the chief," Luna said, moving toward the door. "I know you didn't do it, okay? I may be the only person in the world besides Willis who does know that, but I do."

I leaned against the closed front door. "Are you going to arrest me?"

Luna shook her head. "He didn't say anything

about that. But if the McLemores press him, he might."

"There's something wrong with those people, Luna. I'm not saying they killed their son, but there's something wrong with them."

Luna nodded her head. "The Addams family of Sagebrush Trail," she said. She smiled at me. "Kiddo, listen to me. I'll talk to the chief. I'll try to make him see reason. Willis is a bit of a mover in this town, not a big one, but he's at least a business owner. That means something to the chief. And the fact that he and Willis's father were cronies. . . ." She sighed. "If your name was Maria Lopez and you lived in my neighborhood, you'd have been in jail two weeks ago."

I knew she was right about that. Where I lived, and in a lot of small towns, who my husband was, who my late father-in-law was—all these things were in my favor. My *l*-word gut didn't like it, but I couldn't help being just the least bit grateful for Catfish Watkins's predictable attitude.

Luna patted me on the shoulder and left. I sank back down in the easy chair. Someone had been in my house. The same person, obviously, who'd killed Brad McLemore. Why? Why were they doing this? I'd gone upstairs earlier with Luna, but nothing up there had been touched: just the living room and dining room. I was glad of that, glad that those hands had not touched my children's toys and bed linens; glad those hands had not been in my underwear drawer, touching the clothes in my closet, rummaging through Willis's papers. Sitting in the easy chair, obviously touched by those hands, made my skin crawl. I got up and went into the breakfast room and sat on one of the straight-back kitchen chairs. There was nothing to show those hands hadn't been in here, but nothing to show that they had, either.

I sat and waited. I'm not sure what I was waiting

for. For Willis to come home; for the killer to call again. I knew who had called before. I knew that metallic voice had belonged to the person who'd killed Brad. It was no interrupted burglar or passing serial killer. How much of the things that happened before Brad's death had been caused by him, I wasn't sure of now. Luna had been right: Brad wasn't bright enough to have pulled off a lot of it. And if what Anne Comstock said was true about voyeurs, Brad was responsible for very little of it. The electronic gadgetry with the 911 calls: Brad didn't have the brains for that. Either he was doing this with someone, or he hadn't been doing it at all.

Wait. He had to be the one who'd gone through my jewelry. He was definitely the one standing in the backyard staring at my house.

I leaned my elbows on the table, cradling my head in my hands. I couldn't stand much more. I just couldn't stand much more.

The four of us sat around the dining room table, digesting. The kids had been fed early and sent to bed so that us grown-ups could entertain. Our company was Doug Kingsley and his lady of the moment, Darla Gregory. She was the kind of woman you'd expect to be with Doug Kingsley—gorgeous, sexy, smart. And not particularly humorous. Although I rarely allowed anyone to smoke in my house, Darla had lit up without even asking, using my good china as an ashtray. I didn't say anything about that or anything else.

It wasn't my idea to entertain right now. I thought the timing was a little off—what, with a maniac out to get me or my family or all of us. But Willis had insisted that we have Doug over for dinner. He was priming him for partnership. Partnership with Doug meant an influx of cash, as well as being able to double the workload. Since he'd gotten the Chemco bid, he needed the extra help. And he wanted it on a permanent basis. It would be good for Willis's company. And there were times Willis thought of little else.

We sat around the table watching Darla smoke her after-dinner cigarette. Doug said, "I was telling Darla about all the excitement you've been having, E.J. Crazy stuff."

"Uh-huh," I said.

"Well, you'd think the police would do something," Darla pronounced. "I mean, this is ridiculous. What do we pay taxes for if not to have our homes safe from stalkers and the like? And for God's sake, we just got a stalker bill passed in the state legislature—"

"Before you can put the stalking law into effect, you have to know who's doing the stalking," I said. "As of right now, we don't know who it is."

Darla leaned around the side of the table and hugged me, the smoke from her cigarette drifting into my hair. "You poor thing," she said. She pushed away, keeping one hand on my shoulder while she raised her cigarette to her lips with the other, sucking in and blowing smoke in my face. "You call me the next time something like this happens and I'll just rush right over."

Willis pushed away from the table and held my chair for me, quickly saying, "Why don't we retire into the living room?" Thus covering any retort that might have escaped my lips. I mean, after all, Darla Gregory was certainly going to be the first person I called when the stalker struck again. With any luck, he'd be allergic to cigarette smoke and die in her arms.

Darla didn't offer to help clean off the table, which was okay by me. I had no intention of clearing or washing the dishes. I'd cooked. These were Willis's friends. He could damn well clean.

I sat down on the couch and Doug came and sat down next to me, his arm stretched out behind me on the couch. Darla took the loveseat. My husband, wise man that he was, opted for the easy chair.

"I just can't believe they can't find this creep," Doug said. "Have you demanded they keep surveillance on your house?" he asked Willis.

Willis shook his head. "There aren't enough cops to go around as it is, Doug. And the cops don't do that, anyway. We're on our own." He didn't mention that the cops rarely serve protection on their prime suspect. Though a stakeout on my street wouldn't have been unwelcome.

Doug's hand came up from the back of the couch and rubbed my hair. Grinning he said, "Well, I'll be happy to take the dayshift and stay here with E.J. if you want, Willis."

I got up from the couch. "I'll just go see about dessert," I said, heading for the kitchen.

"None for me, E.J.," Darla said. "I never eat dessert. Or bread." She patted her flat stomach. "Works for me."

I walked on into the kitchen and found a Snickers Bar secreted on top of the refrigerator. I gobbled it down while I made decaf coffee and cut pieces of pound cake, putting them on individual plates and ladling strawberries and whipped cream on top.

When I brought out the plates for the men, Darla said, "Well, I guess I will take just some of the strawberries."

I headed back to the kitchen. "And just a dollop of that whipped cream, dear," she added.

The coffee was ready and I fixed Darla her dessert and poured the drinks, putting the cups and fixings on a tray and took it into the living room. I will admit I thought about accidently tripping and having the entire contents of the tray, hot coffee and all, fall into Darla Gregory's designer-clad lap. But then decided not to. I wasn't exactly sure why I'd taken an immediate dislike to the woman, but I had a feeling my violent streak had more to do with other circumstances than with the woman herself.

The evening wore on and I was a less-than-gracious hostess. Doug and Darla took their leave a little after ten.

As he shut the door after them, Willis said, "Thanks a lot, Eej. Your hostessing skills are outdone only by Lucrezia Borgia."

"You have to clean up. I cooked," I said, heading for the stairs.

He sighed. Then followed me up the stairs. "I'll do it in the morning."

I sighed and turned around, stomping down the stairs to the dining room. "Never mind!" I said, slamming my good china around as I stacked plates to take them into the kitchen.

"Jesus!" Willis said, coming up behind me. "All right. I'll do it now!"

He grabbed a serving dish. I grabbed the same dish, wrestling it out of his hands. "Never mind! I'll do it myself!" I said.

"Like hell you will! You cooked! I'll clean! Give me the goddamn dish!"

I gave it to him, all right. It missed his head by less than an inch as it sailed out of my hand and across the dining room, smashing against the wall and breaking into a million tiny shards.

That's when I fell on my butt on the dining room floor and burst into tears.

The phone was ringing as the kids and I came in from church the next morning. Willis had gone straight to work after the services, and we had taken two cars to accomplish this. I picked up the phone on the third ring.

"Hello?"

"I'm going to do terrible things to your children. And make you watch. Then I'm going to do terrible things to you." The voice was metallic. The same voice.

"Why?" I screamed. "Why are you doing this?"

"Because I can."

The line went dead in my hands.

I grabbed the kids and hustled them back into the car, Graham bitching the entire time.

"Geez, Mom! Conner's supposed to come over when he gets home from church and we were gonna go over to Mark's house and play video games!"

"Later," I said, pushing him and his sisters out the door.

"Where are we going?"

"Your dad's office."

"I don't want to go to Daddy's office! I wanna stay here!" He swung around and headed back in the kitchen door.

I grabbed him by the arm and swatted his butt. It surprised both of us. I'd never spanked any of my children, which is the reason, my parents contend, that they're such spoiled brats.

Graham got very still. "I can't believe you did that," he finally said.

"Neither can I. But now that I know how, I'll try it again if you don't get in the damned car!"

He turned and rigidly walked to the car and got in. He fastened his seat belt while I buckled the girls in, crossed his arms over his chest, and glared out the window. He didn't utter a word the entire five miles into Codderville.

Willis's was the only car in the parking lot. I parked next to it and herded the girls into the building. By the time I got them out of the car, Graham was already at the front door, pushing the emergency Sunday button to let his dad know we were there. It took only a minute for Willis to come down and let us in, but it was a very long minute. I kept looking around me, watching the street, the bushes, the door, waiting for "him" to jump out at us.

Willis let the kids in and I held him back, telling him about the phone call. He, too, looked furtively around the empty parking lot, then pulled me inside the building.

"I think we should call Luna," I said. "The least they can do is put a trace on the line."

"I don't think they do that anymore—what, with caller ID and the other stuff the phone company offers. I'll call Ma Bell tomorrow."

We went to the elevator where the kids were waiting impatiently for us and Willis keyed in his Sunday code.

I kept the kids in the reception room while Willis worked in the big room. I had neglected to bring them anything to play with, and it didn't take long for the girls to get exceedingly restless. Graham, on the other hand, sat in utter silence in one of the visitor's chairs, his legs dangling out in front of him, arms crossed over his chest. Unlike a lot of mothers, I decided I *liked* the silent treatment.

I finally got the girls interested in a game of rock-scissors-paper, but it didn't take long for them to realize that I was beating their pants off. I couldn't help it if they were too young to stick to the rules. We tried singing songs for a while, did a round-robin story, and then finally ended up turning on Angel's word processor and letting them bang away at the keys.

I took that opportunity to call Luna and tell her about the phone call.

"Willis said he's calling the phone company tomorrow and having them put caller ID on our line," I told her. "Then what do we do? Should I call you immediately when I get this guy's phone number?"

"That all depends," Luna said, a weary sigh tinge-

ing her speech. "On one, if he calls again, and two
. . . Pugh, this guy is really high tech, right?"

"Uh-huh," I said, a vague sense of uneasiness beginning to plague me. The thought of getting caller
ID, finding out who this guy was and having his ass
busted, was the first piece of good news I'd had in
a while. But Luna's tone was leading me to believe
that this idea, like any other we might have, would
be useless.

"Well, nowadays, anything that can be done can
be undone. For every action you can take, he can
take a counteraction. Chances will be real good nothing will show up on the readout, and if it does, it
will be for a number that has nothing to do with
our guy."

"How can he do that?" I asked.

"We get catalogues in here all the time with every
gadget imaginable. But you turn the page, and
there's a gadget that will render the other gadget
useless. It's like the old story of the guy who invented the radar gun that patrolmen use. He got a
ticket because of his own invention, then went home
and invented the radar detector. Nowadays, nobody
puts any invention on the market unless they have
the antidote ready to go, too."

I sighed. "So why bother with the expense of
caller ID?"

"Why not? He might be stupid enough not to rig
the call, although I doubt it. Besides, when this is
over, you can always have it taken off."

"When this is over?" I said, trying to push down
the nervous giggle about to escape my lips. "This
isn't ever going to be over, Luna. This is going to
just go on and on."

"Pugh—"

"I gotta go." I hung up and sat in the visitor's
chair by Angel's desk, watching the girls mashing

the keys of the word processor, and feeling like I'd
been feeling for so long: lost, afraid, useless.

Finally Willis finished his work and said we could
go home. We left Willis's car in the parking lot and
all headed home together.

I woke up sweating. At least I wasn't dreaming
about the Lesters any more. The star of this dream
had no face, no form. Just a constant, malevolent
presence chasing me. As I ran and ran. Trying to get
to the children. Trying to get to Willis. Running,
running.

I got up and went into the bathroom and splashed
cold water on my face. The moon was shining
brightly, and I didn't need to turn on a light and
wake Willis just to wash my face. Just to catch my
breath and try to get over the dream. I walked back
into the bedroom and stood by the window that
looked out at the driveway between our house and
the McLemores—the driveway where Brad used to
shoot hoops and stare at my house. The McLemores'
back door opened. My whole body tensed. From the
light of the moon overhead I could see Arthur
McLemore slip out the back door and into the side
door of the garage. While I stood watching, the automatic garage door opener slid the heavy door upward and Arthur McLemore's glistening black Lexus
eased quietly out of the garage, its lights off as it
made its way slowly down the driveway.

I turned from the window and threw my closet
door open, grabbing at some running pants and a
sweatshirt. I'd forgotten all about Arthur McLemore's
last early morning run: the same night I'd seen his
son standing inside my fenced backyard looking up
at our windows. The sight of Brad staring at the
house had driven all thoughts of Arthur's excursion
out of my mind. But this was obviously not an iso-
lated incident. Where was Arthur McLemore going

in the middle of the night? And why? I intended to find out.

The noise of my dressing woke Willis. "What's going on?" he asked sleepily from his side of the bed.

"Arthur McLemore just drove out of the driveway," I said, stumbling as I fumbled on my running shoes. "I'm going to find out where he's going!"

I ran to the door. Willis, usually not able to function well when awakened from a deep sleep, stumbled along behind me as I made my way hurriedly down the stairs.

"What?" he said.

"Willis, I've got to go." I ran into the kitchen and grabbed my purse off the hook by my office door.

He grabbed my arm as I pulled the back door open. "Where are you going?"

"I'm following Arthur. I need to know what he's up to."

"No you're not!"

"Yes, I am!" I pulled away from his grip and ran out the door. "Stay with the kids," I whispered over my shoulder.

I got in the car and revved the engine. How much of a lead did Arthur have on me? Could I find him? Luckily, at this time of night, traffic would be light. I raced down the driveway and down our street. If you turned right on the corner of Sagebrush Trail and Morning Glory Lane, you just got deeper into residential areas. If you turned left, after two blocks, you were on Black Cat Ridge Boulevard, heading toward the entrance to Black Cat Ridge and the highway to Codderville. I was betting he'd turned left.

I saw taillights at the stop sign at Black Cat Ridge Boulevard and the highway. I kept my distance, hoping I had the right car. The car turned right, heading away from Codderville, but as it passed under a streetlight I could see that it was indeed Arthur

McLemore's shiny black Lexus. Keeping my distance, I too turned right on the highway.

If you stayed on the highway long enough you eventually ended up about a mile outside of Brenham, the home of Blue Bell Ice Cream. Somehow I didn't think Arthur McLemore had an urge for Whole Bean French Vanilla. About five miles north of Black Cat Ridge was the Brenham Highway Motor Lodge. The Lexus's brake lights shone bright as he slowed and pulled in to the parking lot of the motor lodge.

I drove on past, just like I'd seen Magnum, P.I. do a thousand times, then doubled back, coming into the opposite driveway. I couldn't see the Lexus. "Shit!" I said, slamming my fist against the steering wheel. There goes my Nancy Drew badge, I thought. But then I saw him, walking around from the back of the lodge. He must have stashed the car behind the building so it wouldn't be seen. I turned the car off and slouched down in the seat, just enough of my head showing so that I could see where he went. He headed for the stairway and went up, knocking quietly on the door of room 210. The door opened and Arthur McLemore slid inside.

I sat there waiting, I'm not sure for what. I wanted to know what was going on inside that room, but I was terrified to get out of the car. I sat there, trying to decide what to do.

But that was answered for me when the driver's side door was ripped open.

Eight

You know the expression "My heart leapt to my throat?" Well, mine leapt to my throat, popped out through my mouth, did a jig on the dashboard, then went back in and sank down to my buttocks. The scream that was trying desperately to escape my lips was suppressed by a strong hand covering my mouth. It took longer than necessary for my psyche and other parts of my anatomy to realize the hand belonged to Luna and, with her other hand, she was busily turning off my interior light.

"Are you going to shut up?" she whispered, squatting down by my side of the car, her hand still reaching up with a firm grip over my mouth.

I nodded my head and she released her hold. "What the hell—" I began.

Her hand moved back toward my mouth and I shut my lips hard, nodding my head to show I was going to indeed shut up.

"You're insane, Pugh, you know that?" she said, the hissed words more a feeling than an auditory sensation.

"What are you doing here?" I whispered back.

"Your husband's brighter than you are. He called me and told me what you were doing. You idiot!"

I pointed toward the door of room 210. "Arthur McLemore's in there. He snuck out of the house—"

"I'm going to have you arrested for terminal stupidity—"

"And this isn't the first time he's done it—"

"You were followed."

That shut me up. I looked around, finally following Luna's pointing finger. A bright red convertible, the black cloth top up, squatted ominously one row back and five cars over. It was a small car, sporty. But most cars look alike to me so it was hard to tell the make. There was a head visible in the car, a male head. The parking lot wasn't well lit: just one light at each entrance to the parking lot, and the front door lights of the rooms.

Luna's body moved upward, her rear end coming to rest on the little portion of seat my bottom wasn't covering.

"Scoot over," she said.

I complied and she got behind the steering wheel while I fought my way over the gearshift lever to the passenger side. "Hunch down in the seat so he'll think there's only you in the car. We'll give him a run for his money," she said. "See how far he'll follow us."

"Didn't he see you come over here?"

She shook her head. "No way. I parked around back when I saw him sitting there and, believe me, I wasn't seen getting over to your car."

She shut the door gently, then started the car up and peeled rubber (badly needed rubber for my rapidly balding tires, I might add) getting out of the

parking lot. We headed back toward Black Cat Ridge.
I scrunched down in my seat, turned so that only
my eyes peered over the backseat and out the back
window of the station wagon, waiting for our pur-
suer to catch up.

"How'd you find me?" I asked as she drove reck-
lessly down the highway.

I saw her shrug her shoulders. "Easy. I didn't see
you between Codderville and Black Cat Ridge. And
your car is rather conspicuous, you know?" (which
it isn't: it's just your normal big, white American station wagon; okay, so there's that one fender we
haven't painted yet that came from a wrecked wagon
of the same make that happened to be red, and there
are pink ribbon streamers on the antenna from somebody's birthday a while back that I haven't taken off
yet, and I'm still using the little donut spare tire on
the right front wheel, but I still wouldn't call my car
"conspicuous"). "So I just kept driving after the
Black Cat Ridge turnoff," Luna continued. "I was
maybe five minutes behind you. I decided to pull
into the motor lodge when I saw the red car go in
without its lights on."

"So that's all it takes to be a detective?" I said. She
didn't answer.

When we'd gone the five miles back to Black Cat
Ridge, with absolutely no one, not even a horny
trucker, on our tail, Luna pulled over. She looked at
me and I looked at her. I didn't want to actually
verbalize what I was feeling—that Luna's idea hadn't
been a particularly bright one—but I think my look
might have given me away.

"It should have worked," she grumbled, pulling
the heavy wagon into a driveway and turning
around.

"You wake up about as well as my husband," I
said. She gave me a dirty look, which I ignored.
"Now where?" I asked.

"Back to the motor lodge."

We were silent the five-mile ride back. Considering my car clock showed a digital readout of 4:37 A.M., and the lulling of the tire-on-pavement sound, I should have been sleepy. But the adrenaline rush was still with me. My body felt as if it had consumed two pots of strong coffee and a couple of Hershey bars. I was wired. I forced myself to calm down as we pulled into the parking lot. The red convertible was nowhere to be seen. Circling the motor lodge, we also discovered the black Lexus missing.

"Well, aren't you the clever one?" I said. " 'Let's see if he follows us,' " I said, my mimic a little nastier than necessary.

"May I point out that I could be happily sawing logs at this very moment if you hadn't decided to go for a joy ride?" Luna said.

"I didn't ask you to follow me!"

"No, but your husband, who has infinitely more sense than you do, apparently, did!"

"And you just do anything Willis asks you to do?"

She slammed on the brakes in the parking lot, so that the wagon was blocking her car. "Look, Pugh, you are the biggest pain in the butt I've ever met. Do you know that? Why I even talk to you after that shit last year—"

"Yeah, well I was right about everything last year, wasn't I?"

"Ha!"

"Ha shit! I was too!" But I was yelling at her back as she got into her car. Doors began to open in the motor lodge from all the yelling. The door to room 210, however, remained conspicuously shut. I slid behind the wheel and peeled more precious rubber getting the hell out of Dodge.

Fog was rolling in as I headed home. I've always had a thing about fog. Before I got to the lights of

Black Cat Ridge, I pulled the car over to the verge of the country road and got out, and leaned against the hood. With very little need for imagination, fog conjures up images of total isolation. Standing there, with only me and part of my car visible to my eye, I could forget for an instance that there was a motor lodge a few miles back, that I had neighbors named McLemore, that Luna was pissed at me, and that going home to my husband was going to be a lesson in abject apologies mixed with incrimination. I could forget about sick cats and bratty children, chocolate kissed with glass and kinky play toys. I could just feel. Feel the isolation, the aloneness. Aloneness doesn't necessarily lead to loneliness. I was not lonely.

Some people fear the fog, not being able to see what could be coming at them. But I know that fog is a two-way street—what I couldn't see coming at me also couldn't see to come get me. I felt safe standing there with my butt leaning against my cooling engine. For the first time in weeks, months, I felt safe.

When exhaustion began to set in, I got back in the car and drove home. When I got there, Arthur McLemore's black Lexus was safely ensconced in the garage. I know, because I peeked—which is one of the nice things about the garages being so close together. It took a couple of jumps to get the angle right to see that his car was there, but it was. There were no lights on in the McLemore house.

My house, however, was ablaze. I went in the back door, bracing myself for the wrath of Willis—not unlike, I'm sure, the wrath of God. I should have known, though, that he'd be asleep. That he hadn't actually gone back to bed showed the major extent of his worry. Willis was asleep on the couch in the living room. The half-finished Afghan I'd started four years before (in one of my domestic frenzies; thank God they don't last long) was draped over his shoulders, the end of it not reaching his butt. I knew he didn't mean to be asleep. I knew he had been truly worried, especially since he'd called Luna in the middle of the night. But we're talking about a man who fell asleep in the labor room with his wife screaming obscenities in his ear.

Being the coward I am, I found a quilt in one of the downstairs closets, covered up the rest of him, turned off the lights, and went upstairs to bed.

I woke up to the overhead light blazing in my face, the bedroom radio turned up almost full blast, Bob Edwards's voice intoning the newest Washington, D.C., scandal on NPR, and Willis not-so-happily banging away in the bathroom.

I had a headache. My throat hurt. My eyes felt like used sandpaper. And every bone in my body ached. I crawled out of bed to the bureau and turned off the radio, then moved slowly to the door, leaned against the wall, and with what little strength I had left, turned off the overhead. I took two steps toward the bed and flung my body forward, hoping it would land somewhere in the vicinity of sheets and blankets. It did. I lay there face down, spread eagle.

Willis came out of the bathroom. "Well, you're alive," he said, his tone implying it was of little interest to him.

"Um," I said, my face working its way deeper into the pillow.

"So nice of you to let me know when you got in so I wouldn't wake up on the couch this morning wondering if you were dead or alive."

I rolled over on my back. "Where did you think the quilt came from? The bedding fairies?"

"I must admit that extreme worry tends to make me less than my usual observant self."

"Willis," I said, sighing, "how long are you going to be pissy about this?"

He looked at his watch. "Until Thursday," he said and left the room, slamming the door behind him.

My children, being the angelic and sensitive darlings that they are, sensed my mood that morning and were more quarrelsome than ever getting ready for school. After Willis's snit, my three darlings' booger jokes, and twenty minutes of "did so–did not," I was on the verge of mayhem. Add to that Bert's newest medical emergency (his hair had started falling out in large clumps whenever Axl Rose looked at him), I was ready for a nice two-week stint in the nearest full-care psychiatric facility. I was not, however, ready for Luna.

She called three times that morning, starting as I walked in the door after taking the kids to school. The first two times I pretended I was the answering machine. Being the quick study she is, she caught on and made me talk to her on the third call.

I wasn't in the mood for Luna's recriminations.

"I'm having you arrested," she said.

"Call my lawyer," I said, hanging up the phone.

She called back. "You're a public nuisance," she said.

"You're the only public I seem to bother."

"Don't hold your breath on that. I'm taking up a petition."

"Is there any reason why you called?"

"Yeah," she said, then was unusually silent. Finally, she said, "Did you happen to get the license plate number off that red car last night?"

I laughed. I laughed so hard I thought my sides would split. She hung up.

After a quick lunch of comfort foods (low in vitamins, high in fat), I went into my office under the stairs and booted up Lavana and Branson. After their mad, passionate quickie (twenty-four pages of adjectives), they had been pulled apart by the scheming Marvela Quicksilver, the local dance hall queen who had the hots for Branson. She'd been whispering nasties in Lavana's tender ears, and Lavana was at the point of actually firing Branson. All I had to do was rectify that situation, get them back in bed together one more time, then have him pronounce his everlasting love and devotion and ask for her hand in wedded bliss. Then this puppy would be in an overnight envelope on its way to New York.

I woke up when my "pick up the kids from school" alarm went off in the kitchen. My face was lying flat on the keyboard and drool had worked its way between the keys. Lifting my head, I saw the screen and read:

> But, Branson, how can you sssssssssssssssssssssss-ssssssssssssssssssssssssssssssssss

I erased my day's work, turned off the computer, and went and picked up the kids.

Willis had called while I was gone (he knows my schedule and knows when I go to pick up the kids; that his action was deliberate is not debatable) and left a message on the answering machine stating that he would be working late and not to expect him home for dinner. I fed the kids macaroni and cheese and carrot sticks (a Pugh household favorite), then stuck a Disney movie in the VCR. Belle had barely agreed to stay in the castle of the Beast to insure her father's freedom before I was drooling away on the couch pillows, one daughter nestled in my arms, another using my hip as a pillow.

When I woke up the credits were rolling and all three of my children were playing tug-of-war with the remote control, competing to be the one to turn the movie off. I grabbed the control and did the honors myself.

"Bed," I said, yawning.

"I think you've already done that, Mother," Graham said.

"Bath," I said, sitting up.

"Baseball," Graham said.

"Brownie," Megan chimed in.

"Broomstick," Bessie said in a fit of giggles.

"Now," I said standing.

"Never," Graham said, running to the stairs with his sisters chasing him.

"Next!" Megan screamed.

"Nowhere!" Bessie said, falling down at the bottom step of the stairs she was laughing so hard.

"Go!" I said, trying hard not to laugh.

All three sat on the stairs laughing so hard tears were streaming down from their eyes. Very succinctly, I said, "You will go upstairs now and take your baths. Bessie, you and Megan may take a bath together. Graham, you may use our bathroom. You will wash with soap and rinse with water. After you get out of the tubs, dry off your bodies with clean towels. Then you will hang up the towels so they can dry. Then you will brush your teeth, using toothpaste. After you brush your teeth, you will wash your faces. Then you will dry your faces. You do not need to dry your teeth, however." This got them going again. "Then, when all that is done and you have each painted your feet blue, call me and I will come upstairs and tuck you in."

Bessie stood up from her second-step perch and put her arms around my waist. "You're so funny," she said. I leaned down and kissed her head.

"Funny looking," Graham contributed, getting up from the step and heading upstairs.

Megan, being Megan, joined Bessie with her arms around my waist. I kissed her too, then sent them upstairs to bathe.

I did not, of course, tuck in Graham. This is not

something one does with Graham. I said good night
from his doorway. I am allowed in to put up his
clothes and to scream about him cleaning his room.
That's it. After I told him good night, I went into the
girls' room and read them a chapter of *The Hobbit*,
which we'd been working on for quite a while. I
tucked them in, kissed them good night, and went
to my room for a quick shower.

When Willis got home around ten-thirty, I was sitting in a chair by the window, my eyes glued to the
McLemores' driveway.

I turned my head when the door to our room
opened. "You and Doug have a good time?" I asked.

"Yeah, we hit every singles bar in Codderville."

Codderville doesn't have any singles bars, but it
does have a plethora of honky-tonks and truck stop
titty bars. I didn't ask, just assumed it had been a
not very funny joke.

Without another word, he went into the bathroom
and started his shower. I went back to studying the
McLemores' driveway.

What was Arthur McLemore up to? An affair was
the first thing that sprang to mind. But what would
that have to do with his son's death? As sneaky as
Brad was, he could have discovered his father's affair
and been blackmailing him. Kill your own son over
a motor lodge fling? It hardly seemed likely. And
who was the person who had followed me in the red
convertible? Was it my stalker? Brad's killer? (who
had to be one and the same).

I sat up hard in the chair. Doug Kingsley had a
red sports car. I didn't know what kind, though. Ask
Willis? *Oh, honey, by the way, I think your wanna-be
partner has been following me around and may have killed
our next-door neighbor. What kind of car did you say
he drove?*

But maybe it wasn't a meeting with a lover. (Arthur's motor lodge thing: keep up, now.) Maybe he

was meeting with the stalker, or someone he hired to kill Brad. But everything still came back to why. Why would Arthur McLemore kill his son? The man was weird, I grant you. The whole family was weird. But that didn't make any of them—even Conner, the bad seed—capable of murdering Brad in cold blood.

I wondered what kind of car Doug's little red sports car was. Willis came out of the bathroom, a terry cloth wraparound covering the lower portion of his body. He was getting love handles. His three chest hairs curled from the damp of the shower. His hair was sleeked back from the shower water, exposing a little more baldness than the last time I'd looked. He didn't look at me. He was aware, however, that I was looking at him. I could tell that because he sucked in his stomach. The terry wraparound had a slit in the side and one thigh stuck out. I stood up and walked over to where he stood by the dresser, running my hand along the exposed thigh.

"My, aren't we trying awfully hard?" he said.

I ignored him, removing the terry wraparound entirely. I took off my robe and pressed my bare breasts against his back.

"Okay, okay," he said, turning into my arms. "It's Thursday."

I pulled the covers up to my chin and curled into Willis's arms, snuggling my head on his shoulder. He ran his hand lightly over my bare thigh.

"I called the phone company today," he said in my ear. "If we wait for them to supply the little readout box, it could take weeks and cost an arm and leg. But I called some electronics stores in Austin, and we can get the readout box cheaper and sooner that way. I'll drive over tomorrow and get the box."

"Good," I said, rolling into him, "and maybe you

could buy one of those things you plug into your phone so you can tape calls, too."

"Actually, that's probably the best idea. When I was talking to the electronics stores today I found out that the phone numbers don't show up on the readout box if the person is calling long distance or from a portable phone."

"What? Then what good is it?"

Willis shrugged, and I told him what Luna had said, about how the guy could probably rig it anyway, so what was the use?

"At least we'd be doing something," he said. "Trying something. I'll go tomorrow to Austin, see what I can find. And I'll definitely get a tape recorder for the phone."

I sighed. "Yeah, at least that way, if we get his voice on tape, maybe Catfish Watkins might concede I'm not the only one out there who's a suspect."

"He'd just say there's no way of knowing it's not you making the calls," Willis said.

I lay very still. Would Catfish think that? Yeah, he would. Would anyone else?

"Do you believe me?" I asked, my voice quiet.

Willis rolled up on an elbow and looked down at me. "Honey, I can't believe you'd ask me that. Yes, I believe you. E.J., I know better than anybody else how badly you lie. I also know you'd never endanger the kids. So, do me a favor, don't ask me that again, okay? It's a given. If you say it happened, baby, it happened."

I reached up and pulled his face down to mine. "I love you," I whispered.

"See," he said, grinning, "I believe that."

I fell back, exhausted. We were getting decidedly too old for doubleheaders. Willis lay beside me on his back, his eyes closed, a stupid smile on his face.

"What kind of car does Doug drive?" I asked.

"A Mazda" came the sleepy reply.

"Oh." A Mazda. Did Mazda make a sports car?

"What kind of Mazda?" I asked.

"We can't get a new car right now."

"I know that, I was just wondering."

"We can barely afford the payments on your wagon."

"I'm not looking for a new car."

"Then who cares?"

With that he rolled over on his side and fell fast asleep.

The next morning I was fighting with the kids, trying to get them in the car to take them to school.

"I don't wanna sit next to Graham!" Megan yelled.

"Then don't," I reasoned. "Bessie, change places with your sister."

"She's not my sister!" Bessie yelled. "My sister's dead!"

Oh, shit, I thought. Anne Comstock time again. We had an appointment after school. I knew Bessie knew this. I was beginning to see a pattern here. Whenever we had an appointment with Anne, Bessie would bring up her birth family, though usually not in such a negative way.

"If Mommy and Daddy adopt you you're gonna be my sister!" Megan yelled. "So you'd better get used to it!"

"I don't wanna sit next to Graham!" Bessie wailed. "He stinks!"

I thought at first Bessie was just using kindergarten blasphemy, but then a whiff of something foul came out of the backseat. It was definitely my son.

"Graham, get out of the car!"

Slowly, oh so slowly, he obliged.

He was definitely rank. This was not the normal "oops, I forgot to take a bath for the last week and a half" stench: a stench I've become familiar with

when dealing with my hydrophobic son. This was
something new. And something dead.

"What is that smell?" I demanded.

"Oh, for God's sake," Graham said, sighing and
leaning up against the car. "You women." Then he
pulled a dead mouse out of his pocket. A dead and
putrefying mouse.

I stepped back from my son. "Take it to the garage
and put it in the garbage can," I said. I went with
him, finding a box to put it in to help curb some of
the odor. We deposited the mouse in the can.

I stood looking at my son. "I'm taking the girls to
school. You go upstairs and take a bath—with soap.
Change your clothes and put those clothes in the
washing machine. I'll wash them when I get back.
Are you listening to me?"

He was rolling his eyes, but he nodded his head,
nonetheless. "What did you plan on doing with that
thing?" I asked.

"Show and tell," he said. The "duh" was only
implied.

"You will be late for school," I said, "and you
will suffer the consequences. I'm not writing you a
note—"

"But, Mom—"

"Go. Now."

"Mother! I'll get a tardy slip!"

"You should have thought about the consequences
of your actions," I said, feeling very parental.

I unlocked the door for him, then locked it behind
him, and ran back to the car to take the girls to
school. I'd never left Graham at home alone before.
He was eight, almost nine years old. Young, too
young. I was opening the door of the car when the
back door of the McLemore house opened.

"E.J.!" Ginger called.

I walked toward the fence separating the
driveways.

"Good morning, Ginger," I said, trying to smile.

"Could you drive Conner to school for me?" she asked. Conner came out of the house carrying his bookbag. Ginger's eyes weren't tracking right. And there was something else wrong. Something I couldn't place. With her hand fluttering near her breast, it finally dawned on me what the problem was: Ginger McLemore's nail polish didn't match her lipstick.

"Sure, Ginger. No problem. I'm taking the girls now, but I have to come back for Graham." At her quizzical look, I just said, "Long story. I'll tell you later. Hop in, Conner." I waved 'bye to Ginger, who waved two Heavenly Mauve fingertips at me while pursing her Cherry Orchard Red lips. I never thought I'd live to see the day.

I dropped the girls and Conner off at school and headed back quickly to my house, mother-guilt making me hurry so as to minimize Graham's tardiness. I guess it was a sign of my lack of sleep the last couple of nights, sitting vigil at the window, waiting for Arthur McLemore's late-night cruises, that it wasn't until I pulled into my own driveway, seeing the house next door, that the thought occurred to me that I'd not only left Graham home alone for the first time, I'd left him home alone with Ginger alone next door: a woman who was obviously, by her new look alone, losing it.

My stomach muscles contracted and I felt bile at the back of my throat. Even without Ginger's obvious problems, I'd left Graham home alone with a killer on the loose.

I slammed on the brake and jumped out of the car, dropping my keys twice in my hurry to get to the back door and into the house. Once I had the door opened, I yelled, "Graham!" at the top of my lungs.

There was no answer.

I walked rapidly through the kitchen, into the dining room, through the living room, heading to the foyer and the stairs. I stopped dead in the living room. A year before I had made this same walk—in the house next door. When I'd turned the corner to the stairway, I'd seen the blood. Child's blood.

My feet were frozen to the wall-to-wall carpet. My knees were locked in position. My heart was pounding in my chest, my breath coming in short gasps. I was seeing spots in front of my eyes. I was still conscious enough to realize I was beginning to hyperventilate. I cupped my hands in front of my mouth, trying to slow my breathing. If I could have walked, I wasn't sure which way I would have gone: up the stairs to whatever horrors awaited me, or into the kitchen for a paper bag: for breathing or vomiting, whichever came first.

I did some counting, some yoga breaths, finally calming myself. My feet began to move. I made my way slowly into the foyer and looked up the pristine stairs. If my life were a Hitchcock movie, there would have been a longshot of the stairs, stretching forever into the mist of the landing.

"Graham!" I called again.

No answer.

I took the first step, the second, my feet pushing their way painfully through the thicker-than-usual carpet, my arms pulling me up by use of the stair rail. The minutes, the hours, the weeks trudged by. Finally I was on the landing. I called my son's name again. There still was no response.

I remember once as a child being dared by my best friend of the moment, Tiffany Anne Miller, to stand on my head for as long as I could. I had bragged that I could do that for an hour. I made it fifteen minutes before the blood began rushing to my head. I had that feeling now. My hands and feet were beginning to tingle and my head pounded to the beat of a very different drummer.

All the bedroom doors stood open, with the exception of Graham's room. I found myself in front of it, my hand on the doorknob. The sound in my head now was like waves crashing on a beach, traffic on a super highway. Loud, unrelenting. I turned the knob.

Graham was lying on his stomach on the bed. Headphones blaring rock music into his ears, one of his ever-present horror comics stuck in front of his nose.

I grabbed the headphones off his head and he screamed, falling back against the wall his bed rested against.

"Jesus, Mom! You scared the shit out of me!"

"Fifty cents," I said, and hugged him hard.

It was nine-thirty before I was back at the house and alone. I booted up Lavana and Branson and, after two grueling hours, was able to guarantee them a life happily ever after, or as long as she could put up with his snoring and he could put up with her monthlies. Now was the worst part: going over and over the book to make sure all the "i"s were dotted and all the "t"s were crossed. Another week at least before the actual mailout of the manuscript. But typing in the words "the end" always did a lot for my self-esteem. I celebrated with some Hershey's Hugs and Kisses and a can of Diet Coke.

I was sitting in the breakfast room, celebrating, minding my own business, all three cats at my feet lest I drop a morsel, when a noise in the backyard drew my attention. I went to the sliding glass doors and drew back the curtains.

The backyard was on fire.

Nine

I threw back the sliding glass door, headed into the backyard, stopped myself, backtracked into the kitchen where I grabbed the portable phone, and ran toward the foyer closet for the fire extinguisher. Passing the big front window that faced the streets, the curtains drawn back, I saw a small flash of red racing down Sagebrush Trail. As my fingers automatically dialed 911, I ran to the window to see if I could recognize the car. It was slowing to make the turn onto Black Cat Ridge Boulevard. It was small, red, with a black convertible top. It could have been the car from last night. It definitely could have been.

The phone in my hands came alive as the 911 operator answered. I told her what had happened. "Uh-huh," she said.

"Did you get the address?" I asked, heading for the closet.

"Oh, yes, we're very familiar with that address."

I stopped, my keen senses picking up something a little out of kilter. She wasn't buying my story. "My backyard is on fire," I said succinctly.

"There have been several false alarms at the address given, ma'am," the operator said.

"Granted. But this one isn't. You get somebody out here now or I will not only sue the county but you personally. What did you say your name was?"

"The fire department is on their way, ma'am."

"Thank you very much." I hung up hard in her ear, I hoped.

I grabbed the fire extinguisher out of the closet and headed to the backyard.

The damage was minimal. Some scorched boards in the fence separating our house and the McLemores', the new fence we'd installed after the fire that almost destroyed our house the year before. A five-foot square of grass was burned, and the two hydrangea bushes I'd bought to replace the ones burned the year before were gone, and half of the beautiful tree with the white blossoms that hung over from the yard behind ours was scorched, possibly ruined.

The kids' new redwood swing assembly was on the other side of the yard and incurred no damage whatsoever. I and my trusty fire extinguisher had everything under control by the time the fire department showed up.

But the fire was the only thing under control. My breathing, my heart rate, and my anger were very much not under control.

I was standing on the patio, leaning my rear against the picnic table, watching the firemen examine the yard, when the fire chief walked up to me, extending his hand to show me something in it.

"Miz Pugh, this look familiar?"

In his hand were pieces of broken glass and some burnt rag. "Not very," I replied.

"Well, I'm gonna have to get our arson investigator

over here to look at this, but seems to me there's a pretty good smell a gas around that part of the fence," he said, pointing toward the fence that separated our home from the McLemores'. "And this sure looks like the makings of a Molotov cocktail. That's a—"

I nodded my head. "I know what a Molotov cocktail is," I said. Images of the flying red car going down my street played in my mind.

"Well, I best use your phone and call my guy, have him get on over here. My boys is fixing to pack it up, but I don't want nobody in that yard 'til the arson guy's gone over it, you understand, Miz Pugh?"

"Sure," I said, leading him inside and handing him the cordless phone.

"If you'll excuse me a minute," I said, grabbed my purse and headed for my car in the driveway.

It was a Miata. Doug Kingsley's car was a bright-red Mazda Miata. With a red hardtop. But didn't Miatas have both? A hardtop and a convertible top? I drove through the parking lot of the Oak Hills Tower, Willis's office building, turned and headed back to Black Cat Ridge. Okay, now I knew Doug Kingsley's little sports car was a Miata. Was that what I'd seen? Could he have changed tops on the outside chance that I'd jump in my car and come over here to check? Was he that clever?

If he was the one who'd been doing all the things that had happened lately, then yes, he was that clever.

Ginger McLemore was standing in the driveway when I pulled up. I got out of the car and said, "Hi."

She was twitching. Worse than that, she was wearing black shoes and carrying a navy purse. "E.J.," she said, smiling brightly. Way too brightly. "There's been some excitement. But then there always seems to be excitement around you, doesn't there?"

I smiled back. "A little fire in the backyard, Ginger. Nothing serious."

"Well," she said, cranking the smile up another level. "Bye." She then wiggled her fingers at me and walked to her back door.

The fire chief and the arson investigator were in the backyard when I went through the gate into my backyard. But they weren't alone. Catfish Watkins was with them.

"Hey, Miz Pugh," he said when I walked in. All three men looked at me as if I were a rotting specimen under glass.

"Chief," I said, nodding at Catfish. "Chief," I said, nodding at Tom Page, the fire chief. They didn't bother introducing the arson investigator, so I just nodded mutely at him.

"Where you been, Miz Pugh?" Chief Watkins asked.

"I had to check something out," I said.

"Uh-huh," he said.

"Did you find anything?" I asked, speaking mostly to the arson investigator.

"Molotov cocktail more'n likely," the arson investigator said, squatting on his haunches in the scorched grass. "Gasoline, whiskey bottle, and rag's all you need. Pow. Real good burner."

"Um," I said. What could I say? That much was already known.

"Miz Pugh," Catfish Watkins asked, "where were you when this here happened?"

"Sitting in the breakfast room of my home, Chief."

"Uh-huh. And what exactly did you see?"

"Nothing. I heard the noise and looked out and saw the flames. That's when I called 911 and got my fire extinguisher."

"Uh-huh." He scratched his clean-shaven face and

looked around the scorched and burned backyard. "Well, now, Miz Pugh, seems like lots of things have been happening around you, don't it?"

"Yes, Chief, it does seem that way."

"Uh-huh. Well, how do you figure this ties in with what else's been going on?"

"I have no idea," I said, leaning nonchalantly against the picnic table. I had no intention of telling Catfish Watkins a blessed thing. I figured he could interpret anything I said as evidence against me.

"Uh-huh. Well, now, Miz Pugh. Looks to me like there's been some damage done here to the McLemores' house, too. I'm just wondering if maybe you decided to teach those people a lesson. I mean, after all, things've been happening, you gotta be getting a little p.o.'d, so you just threw that bottle, but being a woman and all, your arm and aim ain't that good—"

I laughed. I couldn't help it. "Yeah, Chief, I throw like a girl. Arrest me."

Catfish Watkins smiled. It wasn't a thing of beauty. He's missing a molar on the left and the front teeth are stained with tobacco. He scratched his stomach. "Now, Miz Pugh, nobody's arresting anybody. But I surely would appreciate it, Miz Pugh, if things could kinda calm down around here. As a personal favor to me?"

"Are you implying, Chief, that if this person who's harassing me does something else I shouldn't bother calling the authorities?"

"Oh, now, Miz Pugh, nobody's saying that!" He laughed. "Girl, you do tend to take people the wrong way, don't you?"

"Then explain to me what you meant, Chief. I'd really like to know."

"Well, now, Miz Pugh," he said, getting a serious look on his face and scratching his head, "we got us a dead teenager to worry about. And not a lot of suspects."

Part of me wanted to play good citizen—or least play "shove the blame onto somebody else" and tell Catfish Watkins about the red car—but not knowing if Luna had told the chief about our escapade the night before, I decided to keep mute. Besides, he hadn't done much to give me any faith in his ability to ferret out what was happening. He seemed to want to think I was behind everything, up to and including Brad's death.

"Chief Watkins," I said, walking to the gate and opening it. An invitation if ever there was one. "Thank you so much for stopping by."

Chief Watkins gave Chief Page a look and he, in turn, gave looks to the arson investigator and the other fire fighters still in the yard. They began to trail out. Chief Watkins was the last one out the gate.

As I tried to close the gate, the chief leaned back in. "Miz Pugh," he said, his voice low so that no one could overhear him, "you got some explaining to do, little lady. I don't like what's been going on here and, even if you are Willis Pugh's wife, well, now, Travis Pugh's been dead a long time and anything I ever owed that man died with him, know what I mean? You being Travis's daughter-in-law don't cut no slack with me, little lady. One more incident and I'll have your sweet ass in the slammer. You got that, little lady?"

I slammed the gate in his face.

Shaking with righteous fury, with just a tiny hint of total fear, I went in the house and called Luna. "Did you get the make of that car last night?" I asked when I had her on the line.

"Ah, well, I'm not great with cars—" she said.

"Could it have been a Miata?" I asked.

She was silent for a moment, presumably lost in thought. "A Miata's swoopy," she finally said. "Did that car seem swoopy to you?"

"Swoopy?"

"Swoopy. Curvy. Rounded. You know. Jesus."

So I told her about the fire in the backyard, and of the flash of red car exiting the area at the precise time. I didn't mention Catfish Watkins. I figured she'd hear all about that when the chief returned to the station.

"The car you saw was a Miata?" she asked.

"I don't know. I just got a glimpse of it—small and red's all I really saw."

"Then why did you ask about a Miata?"

I sighed. Did I want to bring Doug Kingsley into this? Most definitely not. Finally I just said, "I remembered someone I knew with a red sports car, a Miata."

"And you think this someone might be a stalker and/or murderer?"

"No, of course not. I was just trying to identify the car."

"By accusing your friends of murder and mayhem?"

"I haven't accused anybody of anything! If you will remember, I just said I knew *someone* with a red sports car. I did not name names. Okay?"

"So who drives a Miata?" she asked.

"Oh, for God's sake. Listen, Luna. A red car was seen in the vicinity of my house after a Molotov cocktail was thrown into my backyard. I can't help but think if you'd gotten the license number the other night all this would be a moot point." And with that I hung up.

Willis stood in the middle of the backyard surveying the damage. Finally, after long minutes of his Patton stance (legs spread, arms akimbo), he did an about-face and marched into the house without a word. To say his face was grim was like saying Newt Gingrich is conservative: understatement-city.

My school alarm went off and I went to the stairs,

which Willis had just ascended, and called up to say that I was going to pick up the kids. There was no reply.

We had Anne Comstock after school so I bustled the kids into the wagon and drove into Codderville to Anne's office. I had a minute to speak with Anne before the session, and I told her about Bessie's earlier statement about Megan: *She's not my sister. My sister's dead.*

Anne, as usual, took it in stride. Almost as if she'd suspected such an occurrence. Sometimes I wish I could tell her some outrageous thing one of my kids did and have her go, "Oh, my God, you're kidding!" I don't think that's ever going to happen.

She took Bessie into one playroom, allowing me to take Megan and Graham into the other playroom. These are special rooms for working with disturbed and traumatized children, complete with anatomically correct dolls; which is where Graham always heads first. I sat him down with one of his nastier comic books and got down on the floor with Megan for a rousing game of Chutes & Ladders.

After about twenty minutes, Anne came in and took Megan back to the playroom with Bessie. I took Graham back to the waiting room where I got my weekly *People* fix and he continued his adventures of *Captain Terrific and the Headless Android,* or whatever.

When Anne brought the girls out, I left them under the careful eye of Tess, Anne's receptionist, and went back to the inner sanctum for my brief fifteen minutes of update.

"She's angry right now," Anne said. "And she's taking it out on Megan. The adoption is the last severing of the tie with her birth family. In a way, it will mean they're really gone."

I leaned back on the blue quilted couch and rested my head. "Does this mean we shouldn't go through with the adoption?" I finally asked.

"No. The adoption is necessary—for her and for the whole family. Have you been talking about it with her?"

I sat up and shook my head. "Not recently, no. Anne, with all the crap that's been going with this ... this ..."

Anne nodded her head. "Are you still being harassed?"

So I told her about the backyard, about Arthur McLemore, and about everything else that had happened since I'd picked her brain a few weeks? days? ago. And then, with a rush of mother-guilt, I told her about leaving Graham in the house alone.

"How could I have done that? What was I thinking?"

"Could it be that part of you was trying desperately to live a normal life? A month ago, two months ago, if the same thing had happened, wouldn't you have responded just as you did?"

I shrugged. "I don't know. At this point, Anne, I don't think I know anything."

"Think about it, E.J. Graham elicits certain responses from you by his sometimes outrageous behavior. You were having a typical morning, right? I have two kids, I know what it's like in the mornings getting them ready for school. 'I don't want this cereal. Mom, he touched me! Don't step in the spilt milk! You can't wear that shirt, it's dirty enough to stand up in a corner!' "

I laughed. A typical mother's morning, working or otherwise.

"You were in mother-mode. You were automatically responding to certain situations in a normal, everyday, mother response. Your son was stinking from a putrefying mouse in the pocket of his clothes. What were your normal, everyday, mother choices? Send him to school reeking? Make the girls late to their classes, thereby disrupting not one class but three? Or make him responsible for his actions by keeping him home alone and rectifying the situation by taking him to school late?"

"But these are not normal, everyday mother days, Anne. Things are happening—"

"Not every second. Not even every day. And, let's face it, how much sleep have you been getting a night?"

I shrugged. "Some—"

"Not enough. I suggest you stop staring at Arthur McLemore's house, for one thing."

"But, Anne—"

"All I'm saying, E.J., is that the mind can only take so much. You've been in overload lately, with all that's happening. Add to that sleep deprivation and your psyche decided with the morning's input that life was its normal, chaotic self, and you responded accordingly."

"You're saying I'm off the hook?"

"I'm saying let yourself off the hook."

I felt better than I had in a while as I got the kids into the car and headed back to Black Cat Ridge. I only hoped Willis would be over his snit by the time we got home and that Catfish Watkins wouldn't be waiting on the front steps with an arrest warrant.

It was when we pulled in the driveway that I wondered about having seen Ginger McLemore in the driveway earlier. She'd just been standing there with her black shoes and her navy purse in her hand. Her car had been nowhere in sight, presumably in the garage, where it usually resided. So why had she been standing in the driveway? Her back door leads directly to the side door of the garage. There was no need for her to be in the driveway. Maybe she was waiting for me? For how long? Was it just good timing on my part? Or had someone just dropped her off?

I scooted the kids into the house, deciding I was

becoming unbecomingly paranoid. Willis was sitting in the living room. We had to bypass several suitcases in the foyer to get into the living room.

"So," I said, "what's going on?"

He turned when he saw me. "You and the kids are going to Houston."

All three kids, no doubt thinking of a hiatus from school, let out shouts of joy. I, however, did not. I sent the kids upstairs and sat down opposite my husband.

"You have declared it to be so, is that it, master of my universe?"

He gave me a look. "This is no time to get your feminist dander in an uproar. We've got a prob—"

"My feminist dander is just nifty, thank you very much. But the kids have school, I have a deadline to meet—"

"And we have someone trying to kill us. Or you. Who the hell knows?"

"So they win," I said quietly.

Willis glared at me. "Better they win by us turning tail and running than by a few more dead bodies in the bushes. Someone is throwing Molotov cocktails at our house, E.J. For God's sake!"

I nodded my head. "You're right. But if we take the kids to my mother's—how long do we leave them there? Do you want Graham having to repeat the fourth grade? I think we can squeak the girls through kindergarten, but they have rules in elementary school, you know. Or do we put them in school in Houston? Give my mother guardianship? Visit them on birthdays and holidays? Because it would just be the kids, Willis. I'm not going. I'm not running."

Willis shook his head. "You are the stubbornest woman—"

"Whoever this bastard is, Willis, I'm not gonna let him win."

"Even if it means you being dead, right?"

"I'm not going to die."

He sat there quietly for a moment, his head leaning against the back of the couch, his eyes closed. Finally he said, "I couldn't make it without you, E.J. I'd stop breathing."

I went to the couch and sat beside him, leaning against him. His arm went around my shoulders, pulling me to him. "I won't let him win, you can bet on that," I said.

"I'm not a betting man when it comes to you, babe." He kissed the top of my head. I couldn't answer that. Or what he'd said earlier. How can you answer that? It was like hearing him tell me he loved me for the first time—too overwhelming to deal with. Too much emotion. I wanted to just fold myself into him, bury myself in his strength, let go of everything that had been happening to me. To us. Could we protect our kids from whatever monster was out there knocking on the door? Should we send them away? I didn't know what to do: how to protect them, and myself. How to get our lives back to normal. How to let Willis know I would never leave him. Voluntarily or involuntarily.

"We have to put a time limit on it," Willis said. "Say a week, two weeks. We can get Graham's assignments from his teacher for at least a week, right? So he won't fall behind."

"And at the end of the week?" I asked.

I could feel Willis's shrug. "I don't know, babe. I just don't know."

I nodded my head and got up from the protection of his arm. "I'll go call my mother."

He nodded and I went to the phone.

Graham's teacher was still at school when I called. She attended the same church we did, so we knew her and her husband slightly on a personal level. She said she'd drop off Graham's books (that he'd left in his desk as usual) and his assignments on her way home.

I repacked the kids' suitcases (Willis had managed to shove in all their winter clothes), adding bathing suits and shorts for the warm April weather, and assorted toys. By the time I'd finished that and dealt with the trauma caused by the fact that the cats weren't going too, Kathy Marks, Graham's teacher, had dropped off his schoolwork. Graham, needless to say, was thrilled.

We packed the car, stopped by the store for road foods—juice and cookies—and we were on our way.

My parents live in West University Place, a little city within the larger city of Houston. Because of traffic, it took over two and a half hours to get there.

My mother is one of those women who was born to be a grandmother. As a mother she'd just been so-so. As a grandmother, she was great—if great is an adjective one would use for the spoiling of children. Although her advice to me on child-rearing has always included the adage "spare the rod, spoil the child," she takes grandparenting as a serious experiment in overindulgence.

Mom and Dad live in a huge, red brick, two-story house that had been old when they bought it when I was ten. My mother is heavy into crafts, and the entire house is jam-packed with her latest projects and the results of the ones that came before. There's her paint-on-glass phase of a few years before: Fourteen plates with pictures of fruit on them, prominently in view on a hanging wall display; her wrinkled-paper wreath collection; her ten-square-foot dollhouse totally decorated in miniatures (including miniature wrinkled-paper wreaths and miniature painted plates); her thimble collection; her spoon collection; I could go on, but why bother? You get the picture. My father has a ten-year-old recliner in the living room and a shelf in the garage he can call his own.

Two bedrooms of the five-bedroom house are devoted to grandchildren. One is the female grandchildren room, done in peach and lime green, with an international doll collection (she made the dresses herself, from a kit), stuffed animals, and ballerina wallpaper; the other room is for the male grandchildren, with football wallpaper, spaceship bunkbeds, and model airplanes (this phase didn't last long; we, my sisters and I, believe it was because our dad actually enjoyed that craft). They also have a swimming pool, hot tub, and the gentlest German shepherd ever born. He's swaybacked from grandchildren rides.

I never worried about the pool when my children were staying with my mother. She didn't give them space to breathe, much less drown.

Willis and I spent the night. After the kids were in bed, we stayed up entirely too late telling my folks what was going on.

"Lord love a duck," Daddy said. "Willis, what are you doing about this?"

"Well, sir," Willis said, squirming on the aquamarine loveseat where we sat in the den, "that's why we brought the kids here. I tried to get E.J. to stay—"

My father snorted. "Fat lot of good it does ever trying to get that girl to do anything."

"Excuse me," I said, shooting withering looks in both men's directions, "I'm in the room."

"The other three girls never gave me the kinda trouble that one did," Daddy said, ignoring my existence entirely. "Stubbornist female God ever made."

"Tell me about it," Willis said.

"Mother!" I said. "Make them stop."

"Well, Eloise, it's the truth," said my mother. "You were even a stubborn baby. I'd go to change your diaper and you'd just kick and kick and make the cutest little mad face."

I rolled my eyes and Willis grinned.

Daddy stood up, took a key out of his pocket, and walked over to the gun rack that stood proudly against one wall of the den.

"What's your pleasure, Willis?" he said, his arm waving to encompass his entire collection of armaments. "Handgun for close-in work or long range with a scope?" He unlocked the cabinet and pulled out a beastly thing. "This semiautomatic here has a clip that holds forty rounds. Not real accurate, but does make a nice spread."

I noticed Willis was looking anywhere but at me. I stood up. "Daddy, that's very nice of you, but I don't believe in having guns in the same house as children."

Daddy snorted. "Your kids won't be in your house. They're gonna be here."

Good point, I thought: Graham was only a pane of glass away from the complete annihilation of the planet.

"Besides, girl, I was talking to Willis." Daddy thrust the assault weapon at my husband, who stood up and took the gun, hefting it for weight.

"Real nice, Earl," he said.

"Sweet," Daddy said. "Real sweet piece. You ever done much shooting?"

Daddy knew the answer to that. He and Willis have been arguing our entire married life about the right to bear arms and the merits of the National Rifle Association, a decal my father displays proudly on every automobile he's ever owned.

"Not much, no," Willis answered.

"Well, that's why that piece would do you just fine. All you gotta do is aim it in the general direction and pull—one of them bullets has gotta hit something!" Then he laughed like the joke was funny.

I stood up and took the semiautomatic rifle from

my husband's hands and placed it in my father's hands. "No thanks, Daddy. We don't need that."

Daddy bent down to the bottom of his gun cabinet and pulled out a rectangular piece of paper. "Well," he said, "when this creep comes for you, honey, you just show him this."

He handed me the paper. It was an old, faded bumpersticker that read NEXT TIME YOU'RE IN TROUBLE, DON'T CALL A COP, CALL A HIPPIE.

"Daddy, that's very clever."

"Glad you think so." He was glaring at me. "Willis, you still wear some of the pants in your family?"

"Daddy!"

"Earl—"

My father handed Willis a handgun and a box of bullets. "At least take this. If nothing else, it packs a wollop when you hit 'em over the head with it."

As we prepared to leave the house early the next morning, Bessie tugged at my sleeve. "Are we leaving already?" she asked.

"No, honey. You and Megan and Graham are staying here with Grandma Bernice and Grandpa Earl. Willis and I are going home—"

"Let me get my stuff," she said and started for the stairs.

"No, honey." I caught up with her and sat down on the stairs, putting her in my lap. "Willis and I told you on the way here that the three of you were going to be staying with Grandma and Grandpa for a while. We have to go home—"

"But you're staying here too, right?"

"No, honey, we have to go back—"

"I'm going with you." Her little mouth was set in a stubborn line. I'd seen that same stubborn look on her birth mother's mouth many a time. As I remembered, it didn't come off easily.

"You like staying at Grandma Bernice's and

Grandpa Earl's. Remember how much fun you had here at Christmas?" I coaxed.

"You were here."

"But now you get to act all grown-up and stay here on your own." I smiled real big. It wasn't working.

Graham and Megan had stayed at my parents' house a couple of times without Willis and me but this hadn't happened since Bessie had joined the family. She'd spent the night without us at Vera's house (my mother-in-law), but Vera lived only a few miles from home. This was different. This was the big city and these were people she didn't see on a weekly basis. And, unlike Graham and Megan, she hadn't known them all her life.

My first overwhelming urge was to call Anne Comstock long distance and have her handle this, but I knew I couldn't always rely on Anne to handle every Bessie-problem that came up. In a few short months, Bessie would be legally my daughter. It was about damned time I started acting like her mother.

"Honey, listen to me. Daddy Willis and I have business we have to take care of at home. Because of the nasty fire in our backyard, you can't play back there. Grandma Bernice has a great backyard—with a pool and a hot tub and Muffie" (the German shepherd: who ever heard of a German shepherd named Muffie?) "and we need you to stay here with Graham and Megan and help Grandma Bernice take care of them. You know how Graham gets."

She nodded her head. "Yes. He can be a real pain in the ass."

"You owe me a quarter," I said.

She giggled. "Doesn't count here! Grandma Bernice, can I say 'ass' here without you making me pay?"

My mother, who had been standing nearby,

balked. People do not say "ass" around Bernice Louise Ryerson.

I gave her a look and she said, "Well, I won't make you pay, Bessie, but I don't like that word."

"See how much better it is here? You get to keep your quarter," I said.

Bessie sighed. "When are you going to come get me?"

"In a week," I said. "Just a week."

She hugged me and I hugged her back.

We left the house, the thought crossing my mind more than once that I had no idea when I'd see my children again.

Ten

We stopped on the way out of Houston at an electronics store to pick up the caller ID readout box and save a trip to Austin. The man at the counter explained the apparatus in detail to Willis, all of it going basically over my head or through my ears. I'm the person who used her computer for an entire year as nothing more than a glorified typewriter before Willis made me learn it was capable of doing other things. I'm not even very good with the automatic self-cleaning oven. Technology is not my forte, which is probably why I write historical romance. Who wants to get cosy with a fax machine, or wax eloquent about E-mail capabilities? Not when there could be wild, untamed horses, roaring fires on an open field, hunting lodges occupied by pensive hunks.

Willis charged the box and we left for home. I may have mentioned that I never thought I was exactly cut out for motherhood. That didn't seem to do much to fill up the huge hole left by my children's departure. It's funny the way the little buggers can get to you. I spent the first evening standing at the open door of the girls' room, staring at their stuff, wondering when they'd be able to rearrange the furniture again in Barbie's dreamhouse; or if I'd ever get to replace their pillows again after a too rough pillow fight; wondering if the two cats, sleeping on Megan's bed, now had a room of their own.

I planned on sleeping late the next morning—a rare luxury on a Monday morning—but I awoke when Willis gently shut our bedroom door at seven A.M. I stared at the ceiling, wondering what my mother was fixing the kids for breakfast—Pop-Tarts with some added frosting? Ice cream floats? Whatever it was, I knew they were probably enjoying it more than the oatmeal and bagels they got at home.

I lay in bed another fifteen minutes, then finally got up and got dressed. I was downstairs and in my office, putting the finishing touches on *Reflections in Turquoise,* by seven-thirty. Passing the kitchen on my way to my office, I noticed the readout box, looking like nothing more than a small digital clock, sitting on the breakfast table. I hoped it wouldn't go the way of the alarm system Willis bought last year, which was now stuck away in the hall closet.

By noon I was ready to take the manuscript to the post office. It hadn't taken as long as I'd thought to clean it up and get it ready. Of course, with my mind on so many other things, it may not have been the best manuscript I'd ever sent my agent.

Since I had to go into Codderville to the post office, I stopped by Willis's office to see if he wanted to go to lunch. Angel was alone in the suite.

"Sorry, E.J., you just missed them," she said, smiling at me. "Willis and Doug just left for a lunch meeting with Mr. Dietz from Chemco."

The one thing I didn't want at the moment was to be alone, so I said, "How about I treat you to lunch?"

Angel's eyes got big in her overly made-up face. "Oh, you don't have to do that!"

I grinned. "Come on. Please?"

She stood up and grabbed her purse. "Anything to keep you from begging." We headed out the door.

There aren't a lot of places to eat in Codderville that aren't made of plastic and form a national chain. We went to one of the few that was owner-operated since whenever. The Hut is basically a hamburger joint, but they make great and greasy chicken-fried steak, thick cream gravy, and the crunchiest fries in two counties. I ate the above-mentioned while Angel nibbled on a salad. It should have been the other way around by looking at us. She needed the calories that I could have done without.

"Willis said you took the kids to your mother's?" Angel said.

"Yeah. I hated to do it, but my God, with everything that's been happening—"

"Willis said someone threw a bomb?"

"Molotov cocktail—yeah, a bomb. Luckily it went over the house and hit the backyard."

"Some throwing arm," she said, biting her salad.

Some throwing arm. She was right! How could anyone have thrown a bottle full of gasoline over our two-story house? Nobody could have. Well, maybe Troy Aikman, but I hadn't seen him in the neighborhood lately. Then the backyard had to be on purpose. I said this aloud to Angel.

"Why?" she said, her tiny face scrunching up in concentration.

"Damned if I know. More scare tactics?"

Angel leaned back in her chair. "That could be it. You're right, they couldn't throw it over the house. But the red car—you said that was in the street in

front of your house? So he couldn't have come in
from behind?"

I shook my head. "There's no alley back there anyway. The houses are back to back. He'd have had to
have gone through the neighbor's yard—"

"Were they home?"

"Then why was the car on our street?"

Angel shrugged skinny shoulders. "Maybe the car
had nothing to do with it."

I shook my head. "I'm not really crazy about
coincidences."

"They happen. Besides, you said yourself you're
not positive it was the same car."

"True, but nobody on our street has a car like
that."

"So you don't allow people to visit? To get lost?
To drive though from another block?"

"Why are you raining all over my wonderful
theories?"

Angel giggled. "Sorry. Just playing devil's
advocate."

We finished our lunch and I drove her back to the
office building. We pulled into the parking lot just
as Willis and Doug were getting out of Doug's Miata.
The top was down. Why not? It was a beautiful
spring day. But as I watched, Doug went to the back
of the car and pulled up the ragtop. The black ragtop.

Okay, so I'm the queen of procrastinators. I also
have my moments in the sun as the Queen of De
Nile. I decided to put on my Cleopatra hat and not
think about burned backyards, black ragtops, or my
children's whereabouts, and instead do something I'd
been putting off for way too long: take Bert to the
vet.

With the kids gone and my latest masterpiece
winging its way to the Big Apple, now was as good
a time as any, especially as the clumps of hair he

was losing at a rapid pace were beginning to clog up my vacuum cleaner.

Sue Bromberg is our vet. I'd known Sue for years. We'd been on several of the same committees at church and were den mothers together the two weeks Graham lowered his standards to join the Cub Scouts. He got over that when he found out good deeds were among the order of a scout's day. Sue had seen to the cats' shots when we'd first brought them home and had been the one to tell me that Bert's strange behavior was a seizure.

I put Bert in the cat carrier and took him out to the car. Ernie and Axl Rose watched from the window and, I swear, Axl Rose was sneering. Bert cried all the way into Codderville to Sue's office. We had to wait in the waiting room with a Doberman, a terrified poodle, a long-eared rabbit with a nasty case of diarrhea, and a gorgeous, sloe-eyed Persian that Bert kept flirting with, even in his semi-hairless and permanently fixed condition.

Finally it was our turn in the examining room, where Bert immediately let loose his bowels. I apologized profusely.

She laughed. "That's why God made disinfectant, E.J.," she said. "I spend half my time cleaning up poop, pee, and vomit. It's a vet's life."

After a careful physical exam, some blood tests, urine cultures, and another wait in the waiting room, Sue called Bert and me back in for the results.

"There is nothing physically wrong with Bert," she said, petting him like he had hair. "He has a nervous condition. The best thing you can do for him is keep him away from Axl Rose."

"How am I supposed to do that?" I asked, sinking into the straight-back chair by the examing table.

"Unless you want me to try to find him another home."

I perked up at that. I mean, after all, even Megan wasn't all that crazy about him.

Sue sighed. "It won't be easy though. The best thing might just be to have him put down."

Put down? I thought Axl Rose was already doing a fine job of that. Then the real meaning of the phrase hit me. Have him put to sleep. As in killed. I jumped up and clutched Bert to my breast.

"No, Sue, that's okay. I'll figure out something."

I paid the receptionist and hustled Bert back into the car, where he cried all the way home and lost the rest of the hair on his tail.

As I turned the corner on Black Cat Ridge Boulevard, heading to Sage Brush Trail, Ginger McLemore's Volvo wagon passed me at high speed. Ignoring Bert's wailing, I made a U-turn in the middle of the boulevard and followed. I mean, why just follow the husband? Why not the wife, too?

The sun was shining brightly. I rolled down my window, slipped a Stevie Ray Vaughan tape into the player, turned up the volume to drown out Ernie, and hit the accelerator. Ginger and her Volvo could really move.

We turned right at the main highway, away from Codderville and civilization, toward the motor lodge where I'd followed her husband only last week. I was glad when the Volvo sped past the motor lodge without even a tap on the brake light. The traffic was very light on the country road, so I kept some distance behind her. She came to a tree-shaded bend in the road and disappeared from sight. As I got to the same spot, with a long visible stretch of road ahead of me, Ginger was nowhere to be seen.

There was one road going off the right, and I remembered where it led—to the Brethren retreat. I took the road and drove. When I got to the gate of the retreat, it was closed and manned. I drove slowly past. The retreat is large, and there are some beautiful oaks on the property, but the land was relatively flat for the area and the trees were well spaced. I could see a lot from the outside of the chainlink fence that surrounded the property.

I parked on the verge, shrubs and trees hiding my car from the guard at the gate. On an impulse, I checked the glovebox. Sure enough, there were some opera glasses left in there from taking the kids to a Raffi concert in Houston last summer. My car is a receptacle for all sorts of things. I think in a pinch I could live in it for a week and not die of hunger or thirst.

I grabbed the opera glasses and got out of the car, ignoring Bert's pleas to be taken home. I was sure this jaunt was doing little for his nervous disorder. I squatted down in the grass and bluebonnets that edged the fence, and adjusted the glasses. Finally I found Ginger's Volvo, parked by the gate to the cemetery.

I'm sure I would have found her on my own, but my attention was drawn to three running figures going in the gate of the cemetery. I followed them with the glasses, then passed them. They were running toward Ginger McLemore, who was not exactly standing at her son Brad's grave. What she was doing was jumping up and down on Brad's grave, while simultaneously kicking the headstone. Three pairs of arms, belonging to two men and a woman, grabbed her and dragged her away. When they got to one of the paths of the cemetery, they stopped, the men letting go of Ginger, the woman with her arm over Ginger's shoulder. I couldn't hear, but I could certainly see. Ginger appeared hysterical. The men and the woman appeared conciliatory.

Finally they led her to the small chapel where Brad's service had been held.

I put down the glasses and rested on my haunches. Well, this was certainly interesting, but what did it mean? I'm not sure how long I would have squatted there if I hadn't heard the word "Hey!" screamed loudly. I looked through the fence. A man was standing approximately two hundred yards from me and was pointing his finger directly at me. Then he started running toward the guard shack. I thought it might be time Bert and I headed home.

All three cats had become indoor-outdoor cats within a month of coming to live with us. Nobody could stand having the litter box in the house; better they use the entire backyard. But I found the old plastic tub I'd used as their box and a bag of cat litter, filled it, took that and a dish of water and another of food upstairs and officially turned the girls' room into Bert's sanitorium. Bert needed some R&R and I was going to see that he got it, with plenty of visiting hours. Willis hated the cats, but I'd make sure he went up to the girls' room and talked to Bert a couple of times a day. I was determined to make the cat better. And I wanted Willis to do a little male bonding. Bert needed to know he could take on Axl Rose. We needed to pump up his manhood as well as bind his wounds.

When he was settled in, I left the house, walking the short way around the block to the house directly behind ours. For all her overdone makeup, Angel might have been right. The red car could have had nothing to do with the Molotov cocktail thrown in our backyard. The easiest way to have done it would have been to toss it over the fence from the house behind ours.

Alice and Gary Nelson lived in the house behind us. He was a retired navy commander and she was a school teacher at the middle school in Black Cat Ridge. Their kids were grown and scattered around the country, and Gary had his hand in a lot of business pies. The chances were good that no one had been home the Friday before.

Most of the houses in Black Cat Ridge were built by one of three different builders and they were much alike: traditional upper-middle-class tract homes. Alice and Gary, however, had had their house built to their own specifications. Although it had the same square footage as the rest of the homes in the subdivision, it consisted of only two rooms: one up and one down. There was no kitchen to speak of. They or their beneficiaries were going to have a hell of a time selling that house. The wide open downstairs space was broken in two by a huge freestanding staircase that led to the second floor.

The downstairs was arranged with a conversation area made up of couches and chairs near a freestanding fireplace, and an area off that which housed a desk and filing cabinets. On the other side of the staircase were freestanding bookcases and comfortable chairs and lamps for reading. Beyond that was a pool table. In a corner was essentially a glorified wet bar, with a miniature fridge and stove top and a microwave, and there was a round antique clawfoot table with two chairs also in that corner, for when they ordered in, no doubt.

Alice had shown me the second floor right after the house had been finished and they'd moved in. There was a round bed in the center of the space. One wall was covered with built-in drawers, bookshelves, and hanging racks for clothes. The wall opposite was a series of double doors that held Murphy beds (should the kids come to visit). The only enclosed space in the entire house was the bathroom, which was bigger than both my kids' rooms put together, and it had the largest sunken tub I'd ever seen, plus a shower big enough to hold ex-navyman Gary's last shipload of sailors.

I loved the house. Most of the people in Black Cat

Ridge thought it was an eyesore and a joke. But I loved it. The old radical in me treasured the nonconformity of it, the open spaces, the freeness of it. And I could also understand Gary's desire, after thirty years on ships, to want space around him. And Alice's desire, after thirty years of cooking for four children, to be as far away from a kitchen as possible.

The outside of the house was pink stucco, not a common building material or color for Black Cat Ridge. It was a huge, square pink box with a red Spanish tile roof. The front yard consisted of a three-car garage, Mexican tile walkways, and plants. And since the garage was where the traditional front yard should have been, which was against the rules, the homeowner's association had been noticing and fining Gary Nelson the entire four years they'd been there. Gary gleefully threw the notices away.

I walked up to the front door and rang the doorbell, hearing the chiming of "Anchors Away" inside the house. The door opened and Gary Nelson stood in front of me.

In his mid-sixties, Gary is about my height, five-feet-ten or so, but seems taller because of the way he holds himself. He has a brush cut of gray hair, wide shoulders, and the evilest grin it has been my experience to encounter.

"Hey, Pugh. You burned my tree down," he said as a greeting upon opening the door.

"Hey, yourself, Nelson. And no, I didn't. Whoever threw the Molotov cocktail is the one who burned your tree."

"Damned Russkie. Let me know when you find him so I can sue his ass. Lot of mental anguish going on around here." He grinned his evil grin. "Get your ass in and take a load off."

I followed him inside and sat down in the conversation area. "Gary, any chance you were around Friday?"

"Friday? Yeah, matter of fact, I was. Had me a case of the clomping trots. Didn't leave the barracks all day."

"So you would have seen if someone went into your backyard?"

"Even from the head, where I spent most of the day, come to think of it." He squinted a frown at me. "You thinking the Russkie came through my backyard?"

"Unless Troy Aikman was around and lobbed that thing over our house and into the back corner."

"You're right. He's no Dandy Don Meredith. Now there was an arm. Did you see the Cowboy-Steeler game, October sixty-five? Now that was football."

"The Molotov cocktail, Gary. Keep up."

"Girl, I was in the navy for thirty-five years. I've done enough talking about death and destruction to last two men a lifetime. Rather talk about football."

I stood up. "Well, you've answered my question, anyway. The Russkie didn't throw the thing from your backyard."

He narrowed his eyes at me. "What makes you think he's a Commie?"

I rolled my eyes and Gary gave me his evil grin. I walked toward the door, Gary close behind. "You ever get tired of that wimp Willis," he said, "you give me a call, hear? Alice won't mind a bit."

I rolled my eyes again and left, wondering what Gary would do it any of the women he daily propositioned ever took him up on it. Probably run home to Alice in terror.

I walked back to the house, thinking. How, then, did the Russkie—I mean, the perp—lob the Molotov cocktail into my backyard? From the front, if not impossible, was definitely difficult: no way to get it over the two-story house and into the far corner of the backyard. The house on the left of us was a fortress with huge padlocks on the gates to protect Ellen Carvey's prized lawn frog collection. Who'd want to steal them is anybody's guess, but Ellen has this phobia, and to each his own fear, I always say.

That left the McLemores' house. I should have thought about that from the very beginning. Obvious choice. But why? I shrugged, making a spectacle of myself as I walked down the street. At least I wasn't talking out loud, and the neighborhood should have been grateful for that. But why? Why everything? Why anything? If I knew that, I'd be halfway home to stopping the whole mess. Once you have motive, opportunity and means would just fall into place.

But if the Molotov cocktail came from the McLemores' backyard, who was the idiot who'd lobbed it? Surely they would have done a better job and not scorched their own fence by getting the damned thing further into my backyard. Unless it was Ginger and she threw like a girl. I'd have to check that out. Or—and this ran my blood cold—unless it was Conner. Could an eight-year-old have made a Molotov cocktail? The arson investigator said it was easy enough. Where would he learn how? Even easier than making the damned thing: cable TV. A pop bottle, gasoline, and a rag. That's all he would have needed. And an eight-year-old wouldn't have been able to throw it all that high. An eight-year-old might have missed and scorched his own fence. But why? Why? Why?

And what about the red sports car?

I unlocked my back door and went inside. I went into my office, grabbed a tablet and a pen and sat down at the kitchen table. It was time to get organized. I made a list of all the events that had happened, starting with the 911 calls:

INCIDENT	WHO	HOW	WHY
911 calls	?	?	?
Hershey's Kiss	Brad?	Easy	?
My jewelry	Brad!	Easy	Why not?
The mail	Brad?	Steal it	The check!
Sex toys	Brad?	Buy them	???????
Brad's murder	?????	My hose!	Knew too much?
Metallic telephone calls	?????	??????	????????

I crumbled up the paper and threw it away. Definitely too many question marks. How was that supposed to organize me? It was only making me feel worse, seeing all those incidents laid out like that. My stomach felt queasy. I got up and went to the refrigerator, reached on top and got a Reese's Peanut Butter Cup. Chocolate helps fuel the brain cells. Really.

I was on my third Reese's Peanut Butter Cup and was wondering if there was any Ben & Jerry's Double Nut Fudge left in the freezer when the front door bell rang. I quickly washed chocolate off my face at the kitchen sink and went to the door, peering through the peephole. Wendy Beck, Monique Lester's best friend, stood on the front porch.

I opened the door. "Hey, Wendy," I said smiling.

Wendy smiled back. She was wearing well-fitting jeans and a silky top that showed about half an inch of flat belly. Her hair was windblown, cascading down her back. Ah, to be sixteen and gorgeous again. Okay, to be sixteen again.

"We had a teacher meeting day," Wendy said, "and I don't go to work until, like, four, you know? So I thought I'd come over and give you that information."

For a minute I had to think what information she was referring to, then it dawned on me she said she'd ask around about Brad McLemore. So much had happened since I'd seen Wendy that our meeting had totally slipped my mind.

I opened the door wider. "Come on in. Can I get you a Coke? Some cookies?"

Wendy giggled. "I'm not twelve anymore, Miz Pugh. But a Coke sounds fine."

We went into the kitchen and I popped the top on a soda and offered her a glass. She opted to go with the can straight. We sat down at the kitchen table and she asked about the kids. What could I say? If Wendy's school had a teacher meeting day, then surely the elementary school did too. What should I tell her? I told her the truth.

"Oh, my gawd! Oh, my gawd! This is awful!" she said, all indignant. "How can you *stand* this, Miz Pugh? I mean, I'd be just livid, you know?"

"Oh, I'm livid all right, Wendy."

"Gawd, like those kids didn't go through enough last year, you know?"

I agreed. To change the subject, I asked, "Did you find out anything about Brad?"

Wendy slumped in her seat. "Like not what you wanted, you know? I mean, I asked around and everything, and this one guy tells me he remembers seeing this girl crying and everything the day we found out about Brad dying and all. So I think, like, great, the geek had a secret girlfriend, and I'm like all excited, then when I start digging I find out it was just Tamara Sloan and Tamara has hysterics when we lose a football game, you know? A real easy cry."

"But did you talk to her?" I asked.

"Oh, yeah," Wendy said, taking a long pull on the Coke can. "She tried to make out like she and Brad were big buddies and all, but when I like really pinned her down, it was like she had *one* class with him and he sat on the other side of the room and

they never even *talked* or anything." Wendy rolled
her eyes. "Tamara is, you know, *dramatic*."

"And that's it, huh?"

"Well, I talked to this one geek who said Brad was
in chess club the beginning of the year, but he like
dropped out before Thanksgiving. This geek, David
somebody, he said him and Brad went driving
around one night late in Brad's dad's car, but that
was like *way* before Thanksgiving. And he said all
Brad wanted to do was drive around Black Cat Ridge
and look in open windows."

Surprise, surprise, I thought.

"But he didn't go out with him anymore?" I asked.

"Naw. He said," she giggled, "he said, get this,
'That guy was a real geek,' and I'm thinking, 'Like,
what are *you*?' "

"Wendy, I really appreciate you asking around for
me—"

"Oh, yeah, and I talked to some teachers. But
most of them didn't even *remember* him until I mentioned he was the guy that got it with the *hose*,
you know?"

I thanked her again and we started for the door,
with me asking after her parents and brothers, and
her telling me to keep a, you know, like, stiff upper
lip. I stood at the opened door and watched Wendy
as she walked the half block to her house, wishing
she'd been able to tell me some reason why someone
at the school would have wanted to off poor Brad
McLemore. Some reason that had nothing to do with
me. Poor Brad. Nobody at the school to mourn him
or even remember him. I remembered the funerals
for the Lester family, and the turnout from the high
school of Monique's friends. There were no teenagers
at Brad McLemore's funeral. What made Brad the
way he was? Parenting instantly sprang to mind. Living with the Stepford family was sure to produce

unhealthy children. Was that what was in store for Conner? I hoped not.

The phone rang and I closed the door and moved to the hall table to pick it up, saying, "Hello?"

There was a metallic laugh on the other end of the line. Then a singsong voice said, "I know where the children are!"

Eleven

He hung the phone up before I could say a word. Then my eyes lit on the caller ID box, still sitting in its bag from the electronics store on the breakfast room table. Fat lot of good that did me. I depressed the receiver and lifted it, hitting the speed dial number for my parents. The phone rang four times, then I got: "Hi, this is Earl"—then my mother's voice—"and this is Bernice"—my father's voice—"and we're unable to come to the phone right now. Leave a message and we'll get back to you." Then the long beep. What to say? Whoever it was could have the phones tapped. I was beginning to realize that. Talk cryptically.

"Daddy. This is serious. He knows where the kids are. Take them out of the house. Go to the water place," I said, hoping he'd know what I was talking about. "Then call Detective Luna at the Codderville P.D., 555-4397, and tell her you're there and safe. Go now, Daddy, right now. Take Muffie with you. I love you. Hurry—" But the last part never got on the recorder: the tape had run out.

I laid the phone down and sat gingerly at the kitchen table. My parents owned a beach house in Port Bolivar, a ferry-ride from Galveston. Would Daddy know I was talking about that house? Surely he would. But then I remembered they'd put the house on the market last summer. They never mentioned selling it. Did they still own it? Where would they go if that house wasn't available? To one of my sister's homes? Would The Voice know about my sisters? Where they lived? I picked up the phone again and called Willis, telling him simply to come home. I wasn't about to say anything more on a telephone. Maybe ever. My next call was to Luna. I told her to get her butt to my house pronto. I hung up, not giving her a chance to argue with me.

Then I went next door. It was time to confront Ginger McLemore. She may not have any idea what was going on, but I was mad and scared and I needed to take it out on somebody. Ginger was handy. Besides, her earlier activity at her son's grave made me think her capable of anything, including endangering *my* children. I rapped smartly on her back door—okay, I pounded on it like I was attempting murder with a blunt object—and waited. No response. I pounded some more. Nothing. I moved to the garage and got up on tiptoe to peer in the window. The Volvo wagon was in the garage. She was home. She knew it was me and she was hiding out.

I ran to my house, taking a key ring out of my Tupperware cabinet. The key had been given to me by Terry Lester. I'd never thought about throwing it away or letting Ginger know I had it. I only hoped they hadn't had the locks changed when they moved in. I ran back out the door and used the key on the McLemores' back door. It worked.

I thrust the door open and yelled, "Ginger! Ginger, it's me, E.J. Where are you?"

There was no reply. In my fury to get at the woman, I shoved a kitchen chair out of my way, heading for the door that led into the dining room. It took me two or three seconds to traverse the dining room and foyer and head for the living room. Ginger was there. She wasn't looking her best. She had a runner in her hose, her lipstick that still clashed terribly with her fingernail polish was smeared, her hair was disarrayed, and she was lying in a most unbecoming heap in the middle of the living room floor. Which pissed me off even more. How dare she be down before I had the chance to knock her down?

I knelt beside her and felt her pulse. It was weak but there. A bottle of tequila—the kind with the worm in the bottom—sat on the coffee table, along with a bottle of pills. I picked it up: Valium, 5 mg. There were no pills in the bottle. I assumed they were all in Ginger at the moment.

I found a phone in the kitchen and dialed 911, giving them the McLemores' address. (Funny, they didn't balk at coming to *their* house.) Then I went back into the living room and tried to wake Ginger. I'm a big woman, as I might have mentioned. Ginger wasn't. I was able to get her to her feet, although she was mostly dead weight. I dragged her to the three-quarter bath off the living room, under the stairs, and splashed cold water on her face. Then I did something only a mother used to wiping dirty butts and suctioning snot would be able to do: I stuck my finger down Ginger's throat.

After three tries and three gagging sounds, she began to heave. When she got as much up as I thought possible, I pulled open the sliding glass door of the shower stall and tugged her into it, turned on the cold water full blast, and shook her, yelling at her to wake up. Finally she turned one bleary eye at me, smiled, reached a finger up and tugged at my hair.

"You have such funny hair," she said. "Just like a carrot."

Then her head dropped again. That's when the doorbell rang. I sat her up and turned off the water, running, dripping wet myself, to the front door.

The paramedics had arrived. I showed them where Ginger was, gave one the bottle of pills and the remnants of the tequila bottle, and leaned against a wall. Things were not going well.

That's when I remembered my frantic calls to both Willis and Luna. I left Ginger to the able ministrations of the paramedics and rushed out of Ginger's house.

Something strange had happened to the sky while I'd been with Ginger. It was around five o'clock, too early even in these days of pre-daylight savings time, for the sky to get dark. But the entire sky to the east, north, and south, was a brilliant navy blue. To the west the sky was golden, a gold light shining over everything. People stood out on their front steps, some interested in the goings on of the paramedics, but most were staring at the sky. Great slices of white streaked through the navy to the east, and thunder reverberated. Yet the golden light still bathed everything in its eerie glow. Incongruously, I thought how much I'd like to share God's colors with my children.

Willis and Luna were both standing in my front yard, looking alternately at the ambulance and the sky.

"Did you kill her?" Luna asked by way of greeting.

"Didn't get the chance. She OD'd on booze and tranqs."

"Well, I'm really sorry and everything," Willis

said, "but is that why you dragged me out of a meeting?"

Good neighbor Sam in all his glory. "No," I said. "I got a phone call from Mr. Metallica. He said he knows where the kids are."

Willis and Luna turned as one and rushed in the house, with me following, still dripping water all over the place.

"I called my parents," I said to their backs. "They weren't home but I left a message."

"We've got to get to Houston," Willis said.

"I told my parents to call you," I told Luna, "when they got somewhere safe. I was afraid this line might be bugged."

Luna nodded. "Good thinking," she said. She rubbed her head. "I better get back to the station in case they call." She turned and looked at Willis. "If E.J.'s folks are moving the kids, it won't do you any good to go there. And in this weather it would be dangerous, to say the least. Besides, this might just be a trick to get you to go to the kids so he can follow."

Willis sank into the couch and covered his face with his hands. "Jesus Christ, what's going on? I can't take much more of this!"

I rested a hand on my husband's head and turned to Luna. "Let me know when you hear from my folks," I said.

She nodded and was out the door.

Willis and I stood for a while at the front window, looking at the sky. The golden glow began to fade. The stillness of the landscape began to fade with the glow. The wind picked up. Tiny wind spirals grabbed at leaves left over from the previous fall, whipping them into a frenzy. Then the rain came. Great heaping gobs of it. Hail, first the size of peas, began to bounce of Willis's car in the driveway. The peas grew to walnuts, the walnuts to lemons. It was

a sign of the extraordinary times we were living in
that Willis didn't even glance at his car, ignoring the
damage the hail would do. When your children
could be in trouble, it's amazing how little material
things can mean.

The call came at seven-thirty that evening. The tor-
rential downpour and hail had stopped, slackening
off to a dull, steady rain. The wind had stilled, letting
the rain fall straight down in a gentle spring shower.
Luna had stayed overtime waiting. When she called
I told her to hang up and I'd call her right back.
Willis and I got in the wagon and drove to the gro-
cery store where there were pay phones. Sloshing
through puddles, I dialed Luna at the station.

"Everybody's okay," Luna said first. "I talked to
your dad. He said he didn't think the house in Port
Bolivar was a good idea because he was on record
as owning it. And it's true. We don't know how good
this guy is, but it's best to assume he's real good.
But everybody—your mom, the kids, and the dog—
are at an undisclosed hotel in an undisclosed city
somewhere in the state of Louisiana."

"Louisiana?" And I'm sure they were there with
all the guns left in Daddy's arsenal. The kids were
safe, but I'd worry about the room service attendants
being blasted from here to the Gulf of Mexico.

I gave the phone to Willis so Luna could tell him
what she'd just told me.

After he'd put the phone down and gotten into
the car, I asked, "How about a trip to Codderville
Memorial? I think I'd like to check on Ginger
McLemore."

He nodded and started the car.

Conner McLemore was sitting on a bench outside
his mother's hospital room, his little feet dangling as
he kicked them back and forth, humming a patriotic
tune. He smiled brightly upon seeing us.

"Hi, Mr. and Mrs. Pugh. It's so nice of you to come see Mother. And I appreciate you not bringing flowers. The room can get so crowded that way."

The little shit. "Where's your dad?" Willis asked.

"He's inside with Mother. She's still asleep, but the doctors say she's going to be just fine." He beamed at us.

Willis knocked on the door and opened it a crack. I peered over his shoulder as he bent to look in the room. Arthur McLemore, who had been sitting at his wife's bedside, reading a Robert Ludlum novel, stood and walked toward us, also beaming. Willis and I moved into the room.

Arthur walked up to me and took me in a bear hug. "E.J., E.J., E.J.!" he said. He held me away from him and again beamed at me. "How can I say thank you? You saved Ginger's life!"

Just so I could take it, I thought, but didn't say so. "Well, Arthur—" I started, but didn't get far because he pulled me to him in another embrace.

Releasing me, only to grasp onto my shoulder and pull me to him from the side, he beamed at Willis. "Do you have any idea what a jewel you have here, Willis? Any idea?"

"Arthur—" Willis began, but Arthur released me and grabbed Willis in a bear hug. I guess it was Arthur's way of thanking Willis for being smart enough to have married me in the first place. And, let's face it, he did deserve something for that.

Willis managed to disentangle himself from Arthur, and I stood far enough away so I couldn't be grabbed again. I asked, "What do the doctors say?"

"Touch and go for a while, but your making her vomit when you did may have saved her, E.J. They think she's going to pull out of this just fine."

"Arthur, I need to tell you something I saw today—"

He came to me with his arms outstretched. He

managed to grab Willis on the way with one arm tightly across his shoulders and his other arm around mine, turning me toward the door. "I really appreciate you both coming to see Ginger like this." He shoved Willis out the door and turned me toward him, two big hands clasping my shoulders. "You are a living angel, E.J., you really are." He kissed me smack on the lips and pushed me out the door, closing it quietly behind him.

Willis and I stood in the hall staring at the closed door. We looked at each other, then over at Conner sitting on the bench. He smiled brightly and wiggled his fingers. " 'Bye," he said.

The rain had slackened off and the sky was clouded and dark by the time we got home. The phone was ringing when we unlocked the door to the house. I beat Willis to it. My father's voice said, "Give me a secured phone number."

Thinking quickly, and remembering the key still in my jeans pocket, I gave him the McLemores' number. "Five minutes," Daddy said and hung up. I couldn't help thinking he was having a lot of fun with this.

Willis and I rushed over to the McLemores', knowing the house was empty. I guess that could have been considered breaking and entering, except all we were really doing was entering.

In five minutes precisely the phone rang. The McLemores have a speaker phone in the kitchen, so I pushed the button allowing Willis and me to both speak and listen.

After my hello, Daddy said, "What the hell is going on there, Eloise?"

I told him exactly what the metallic caller had said.

"Well, the kids are safe," he said.

"Earl, where are y'all?" Willis asked.

"That's on a need to know—"

"Daddy!"

"You sure this is a safe line?"

I thought about it. There was no reason for the McLemores' phones to be tapped. Even if one or all of them were responsible, they wouldn't bug their own phones.

"Yes, Daddy," I said,. "it's a safe line."

"We're at the Fontainebleu in New Orleans."

"With the dog?"

I heard my father's evil chuckle over the line. "Graham put on some sunglasses and we told them he was blind and Muffie was his seeing eye dog!"

"How are the kids taking this?" I asked.

"They're having a blast. We told them we were taking a vacation. It's muggy as hell here in the spring, and there sure are a bunch of weirdos, but we're having a great time."

"Earl, we'll send you some cash—"

"Don't worry about it. That crazy might catch you mailing it. Besides, my Visa Gold's got another twenty thousand dollars left on it. That should last your mother at least two or three days, Eloise!" he said, laughing.

"Daddy, thank you so much—"

"Ah, hell, girl, your mother and I haven't had a vacation in years. All my fault. I keep saying me being retired's vacation enough, but you know, traveling can be fun. Even with three kids like yours!"

"Kiss 'em all for me, Daddy."

"Tell 'em I love 'em, Earl."

With that we hung up, both of us staring at the McLemores' formica table top. Finally we looked at each other. "They're safe," Willis said.

"Until the hotel realizes Graham isn't blind."

The next day Willis and I barged unannounced into Catfish Watkins's office. He was sitting at his desk, feet on the desk top, leaning back, tying a fishing fly. Ah, the tortures of the public servant. His feet came down in an audible thud when we came through the door.

"Well, hey, Willis, Miz Pugh," Catfish said, trying to paste a smile on his face.

Willis leaned forward, hands on Chief Watkins's desk. Willis is a big man and he has been known to intimidate. He was doing his damnedest now. "Listen to me, Catfish Watkins, and you listen good. Just between you and me, my daddy got to drinking a little too much last time he and I went fishing, about four months before he died. And you know my daddy when he had a few—he loved to talk. And he told me this story all about him catching you at your hunting lodge with Ralph Podin's wife—"

Catfish was standing up. He laughed heartily. "What can I do for you, Willis?"

Willis smiled. "My wife and I have had to take our kids out of town because of all the harassment that's been going on. Whoever is doing it phoned E.J. yesterday afternoon late and told her he knew where the kids were. My kids are now in hiding in another state, Catfish. You know what that feels like? Having your kids in hiding?"

"My gawd, Willis, I didn't know anything of this sort was going on—"

"Like hell you didn't," I interjected. Willis gave me a look. I shut up.

"You think it's damned easy to blame all this on E.J. because you haven't troubled to look for anybody else," Willis said. "Well, you'd damn well better start looking. And I want someone from your department in my house within the hour to sweep for bugs and to keep an eye on what's left of my family. I have a caller ID box I'm installing today, and if that asshole calls again, I want him caught. Do I make myself perfectly clear, Catfish, or do I need to have Brune Duff give you a call?"

(Brune Duff was a state-known defense attorney

who lived in Codderville. His name did the same thing to cops that names like Racehorse Haynes and F. Lee Bailey did.)

Catfish came around the desk and attempted to put an arm on Willis's shoulder. Willis shook it off. "Now, Willis, calm down," Catfish said. "I certainly see where you're coming from. I'll have a technician out to your house within the hour. You have my word on that."

Willis turned around abruptly and walked out the door. I gave Catfish Watkins a Ginger McLemore two-finger wave and followed my husband.

Once in the car, I said, "So, tell me all about Catfish Watkins and Ralph Podin's wife."

Willis rolled his eyes. "I can't tell you more than this: Fishing cabin, dead of night, and someone was handcuffed to the bed wearing a lace nighty—and it wasn't Lu Ella Podin."

"What was she wearing?" I asked between giggle fits.

"Daddy said it looked a lot like uniforms he saw in Germany during World War Two."

Thirty minutes after we got home, Luna brought the Codderville P.D. technician over to our house to sweep for bugs. There were two: one in our telephone in the bedroom, and one in the kitchen phone. The new portable was clean. He supervised while Willis set up the caller ID box.

Juan, the technician, installed a hotline phone that I was to use if I had Mr. Metallica on the line. All I had to do was pick up the hotline phone and I would be instantly connected to Juan or someone in his department. The hotline phone could pick up any conversation in the room and, by way of a connecting line between it and the wall phone in the kitchen, pick up the conversation on the other line. I could make calls out on any line, but I should only pick up calls on the kitchen line.

"Probably won't do any good, though," Juan said. "Alls he gotta do is use a portable or cellular phone and the ID won't pick it up."

With that happy thought, he and Luna left, followed closely by Willis. I took the opportunity to call the Fountainebleu and tell my parents our phones were clear. Then I talked with each of the children.

"How's your blind act coming?" I asked Graham.

"Not so good," he told me. "One of the bellhops caught me playing pinball and said, 'I thought you were blind!' so I pretended I couldn't hear him and Grandpa said, 'Oh, no, he's deaf. That dog's for the hearing impaired!'"

"Did he buy it?" I asked.

"Naw. He just winked and this morning he brought Muffie up a steak bone and Grandpa tipped him a fifty."

I groaned inwardly. We'd have to pay my parents back for all this, and the tab was going to be astronomical.

I got off the phone and worried. I've always been a believer in the old adage that you get what you ask for. I'd worked with handicapped children for a short while before my own came along, and I hated Graham "pretending." It reminded me of right before he was born. While pregnant, I'd told a joke somebody had told me: "What does a harelip cow say?" The answer is "Moof." Well, I thought it was terribly funny. I told it a lot. When I was eight months pregnant, I was in a store and saw a mother holding a small baby with a harelip. I never told the joke again. And when Graham was finally born, I didn't ask how many toes and fingers he had, I just asked to check his mouth.

I didn't think God would strike my son blind or deaf for his pretense, but I'd have to have a talk with Graham when he came home, of that much I was certain.

When he came home: when they all came home. But when that would be I had no idea. How long would my children be gone? How long would Bert have full reign of the girls' room?

I decided to shut off my brain for a while and go upstairs and primp. We had a party that night, as inappropriate as that might seem. But this was one we had to attend. The Chemco tenth anniversary party: a semiformal affair at the old Codder Inn.

Willis got home early, around five, to take his shower and get ready. My naturally curly, carrot-red hair had calmed down admirably for the affair, which well it should with the amount of mousse and curling iron time I'd given it. I put on black underwear (bra, panties, slip, and hose) and slipped into my "good" dress. I've had it for four years and it's one of those wonderful dresses I can wear to any dress-up occasion any time of the year. It's black, naturally, made of raw silk, with three-quarter sleeves, a jewel neckline, and A-line skirt. In the winter I dress it up with a velvet blazer. But, as it was mid-April and warm, I wore it with just my pearls. I slipped into my black suede pumps and inspected myself in the mirror. I was gorgeous.

Willis came out of the bathroom naked, demanding to know where his tie was. He only has one. Being his own boss, he'd set a dress code early on that eschewed ties and depended heavily on blue jeans. Secretly I thought that was one of the main reasons he wanted Doug to become his partner. Doug was tie-rich and could be the one to entertain the clients when dress-up was required.

But tonight there was no getting out of this dress-up occasion. Both his and Doug's presence were "requested." I was getting the distinct impression that when Mr. Dietz requested, you asked how high.

I found Willis's tie and went in search of his cuff links. I found them holding on the legs of a bedraggled teddy bear in the girls' room. His good black socks were in Graham's room, draped over his headboard. His slacks, shirt, and blazer were in his own closet. Will wonders never cease?

We congratulated each other profusely on how gorgeous we were and headed out to the car.

The anniversary celebration was in the old Codder Inn. Since it is the only Codder Inn, I don't know why it is always referred to as the "old" Codder Inn, except possibly because it is terribly old, by Texan standards. Built in the late 1880s, it's made of native Texas granite, just like the capitol building in Austin. It's only two stories tall and is no longer used as an inn. There's a restaurant on the ground floor, along with some meeting rooms. The entire second floor is meeting rooms and ballrooms. The two ballrooms, which are separated by a sliding partition, had been made into one large room for the Chemco celebration. A band was set up at one end and a huge, beautiful buffet was set at the other. Everybody there looked almost as good as Willis and I.

Doug Kingsley came over to where we were standing by the entrance. Okay, Doug looked better than anybody else there, but when didn't he?

"Hey, Eej, you look great!" he said, grinning at me. I smiled demurely. Never argue with a man when he's right. "I got us a table over there," he said, pointing. "Come on."

We followed him to a table for six near the dance floor. The other three occupants were Doug's date of the evening, a woman he introduced as Amanda Griffin, a petite blond with a vacant look in her eyes, and Chemco VP David Rutherford and his wife Cathy. David was big, loud, and full of himself, while Cathy was soft-spoken, shy, and an absolute knockout. The perfect couple.

Looking around the room, I spotted Angel sitting

at a table at the back with three other young women. I waved and she smiled and waved back.

The food was your usual expensive party buffet: boiled shrimp and crab legs, crudités, baby quiches, exotic cheeses with water crackers, pot stickers, tiny egg rolls with plum sauce, guacamole with chips, tamales, and much more. I took a little bit of everything, then went back for a little bit more. The champagne was flowing freely—literally: there were champagne fountains all over the place, and Willis had been named designated driver. I refilled my glass liberally.

Mr. Dietz made his introductory speech around eight o'clock, followed by a speech from David Rutherford, who ended by introducing Willis and Doug. Both stood up and Doug deferred to Willis, who thanked everyone for something (I wasn't sure what) and said how proud he was to be part of the Chemco "family." I didn't vomit. I was proud. If anyone in that room had ever heard what he had to say in private about "Daddy" Dietz, they might not have been able to hold down their urge to regurge.

After the speeches, the band started playing, and couples, led by Mr. Dietz and what one could only assume was his second or third wife (he's mid- to late-fifties, bald and suntanned; she was maybe twenty-five, a bottle redhead, and had what one could only assume were very expensive breasts), went onto the dance floor. Willis led me out and we danced cheek to cheek to Nat Ramsey and the Raiders' rendition of "Strangers in the Night." Old Blue Eyes would rest easy tonight.

We were walking back to the table when the band started their next song, "When a Man Loves a Woman." Doug grabbed my hand and swung me out on the dance floor. I've always found that song an especially nice one to dance to, but only with someone who loves me.

Doug moved me into the middle of the dance floor, holding onto me tightly. I assumed he was the tiniest bit drunk, and tried to gently push myself away.

"Hey, now," he said, pulling me back. "I like you close. You've got great tits."

What do you say? Thanks? "Thanks," I said.

"I love Rubens' paintings," he breathed into my ear. Why is it that every man who has ever hit on me since I gained weight has used the old Rubens line? Was there never anyone else in the history of man who appreciated us full-figured gals?

"I could really make you happy," he said, again breathing in my ear.

"Uh-huh," I said, shaking my head from the tickle of his breath.

"You and me together, Eej, we could bring down the rafters, huh?"

"Doug, I think—"

"Let's blow this pop stand," he said, breaking away from his hold on me and dragging me by the hand through the throng of dancers. "My car's right outside," he said, pulling me close. "Five minutes to my apartment and ectasy."

I grabbed my hand away. "Get real, Doug. You're not my type."

Too much champagne, too much input over the last few weeks, whatever. My statement was said entirely too loudly. Everyone on the dance floor, including Mr. and Mrs. Dietz, turned in our direction.

I stomped back to the table. Willis had obviously heard the commotion. He was standing as I made my way back. "Get me out of here," I said.

The drive home was in total silence, punctuated by the occasional "What exactly did he say?"

"Nothing."

"Well, shit."

Ten minutes of silence. Then, "But what did he say?"

"It's not important."

Ten minutes more of silence and we were home. We went to sleep with our backs to each other, neither saying very much more than "good night."

I was sleepy, but sleep wouldn't come. My mind was in a turmoil. Doug Kingsley. Red Miata. Black ragtop. That was no gentle come-on. That come-on had been rather insistent. A smaller woman might not have gotten away from him without help. But there had been a roomful of people there. All I'd have had to do was holler and someone would have helped. My God, my husband was only a few feet away. But still I felt dirty. Violated. I got up around three in the morning and took my second shower of the night.

Willis left sometime early in the morning. I slept through it. I didn't get up until almost eleven, bleary-eyed from lack of sleep and too much champagne. I fixed coffee and read the *Codderville News-Messenger*. Not much happening in Codderville. The Chemco anniversary party had been covered. Thank goodness there was no mention of my mini-scene.

I was trying to figure out what to do with myself for the rest of the day that loomed ahead of me when the doorbell rang. I went to the door, peeking through the peephole to see who was there.

Doug Kingsley stood on my front porch.

Twelve

Funny, but Doug didn't look as good to me as he used to. Now he just looked kind of smarmy. A little too much—like one of the Chippendale dancers.

I opened the door against the chain lock and said, "What do you want?"

He grinned sheepishly. "Just came to apologize," he said. He stuck his hand out. In it were a bunch of wild flowers, all tied with a pretty pink bow.

"No, thanks," I said.

He let his arm with the flowers drop to his side. He got a sincere look on his face. "E.J., I'm really sorry. Can we just talk for a minute?"

"I have nothing to say to you, Doug."

"Just let me in a minute, please. I really need to apologize."

I sighed. I needed to talk with him too, but I'd be damned if I let him in my house. "Get off the porch. Walk to the end of the sidewalk," I said.

He did as I asked, standing close to the driveway. I unlatched the chain lock and opened the door. I stepped out on the porch, closing the door behind me.

Rain clouds were building up again to the east and a smell of Houston was in the air—a stench of refineries and too many cars in too little space.

Doug took two steps up the sidewalk. "That's close enough," I said. "Now. What do you want?"

He spread his arms out imploringly. "I'm supposed to holler this? Can't I get closer?"

"No."

He sighed. "Okay. Look. I was drunk. I shouldn't have come on to you like that—in public and all—"

"As opposed to private?"

He smiled. "Well," he said, spreading his arms wide again.

I started to turn around toward the door.

"E.J., look," he said, taking two steps closer.

I glared at him.

He moved closer.

"Stop or I *will* scream, and believe me, I have the lungs for it," I said.

He stopped. "You know something's been going on between us—" he started.

I frowned. "Oh, really? And what exactly is that, Doug? Have we been having an affair that slipped my mind?"

"E.J., the chemistry. It's there, you—"

"Nope. Sorry. No chemistry. And even less biology. Maybe a little geography—"

"Come on," he said, moving closer. I opened my mouth to scream and he took two steps back.

I folded my arms over my chest. "Truth?" I said. He nodded. "I found you mildly attractive when I first met you. And that's okay. I can do that. I also find Marty Zimmer, the pharmacist at the drugstore, mildly attractive. But I'm in love with Willis. I always have been and I always will be. I find infidelity morally reprehensible as well as stupid in this day and age. I don't want to sleep with you, Doug. I don't even want to neck with you. And after last night, I'm finding very little attractive about you."

He gave a grin that looked a lot more like a sneer. "Pretend all you want to, E.J. But I know all about you—"

"Oh, you do?"

"Yeah, I do and—"

He was interrupted by a car pulling into the McLemores' driveway. "You want to leave now, Doug? I really don't want to have to explain to Willis why you're here," I said.

"Like he'd care?" He snorted a laugh but headed for his Miata.

I'd wanted to ask him questions like: where he was the night I followed Arthur McLemore to the motor lodge, and if he knew how to make a Molotov cocktail, but the conversation never seemed to go in the direction I wanted. And I would like to have known what the hell he meant by that last line, Why would Willis care? What did he know that I didn't know?

But now my attention was drawn to another quarter: Arthur McLemore was bringing Ginger home from the hospital. I crossed the driveway, trying to excuse her appearance. I knew Arthur must have brought her the clothes she was wearing, and I also knew she'd just gotten out of the hospital. Her hair probably hadn't been washed in a day or two and it hung limp and lifeless on her head, and although she *had* put on makeup, she had forgotten to do one eye, giving her a rather cockeyed appearance. The pale yellow cotton sweater and broomstick skirt I'd seen her wear before, but not with the oversized sweater tucked halfway into the skirt and the skirt hiked up so far in back that she looked as if she was about to tumble over.

"Hi, Ginger," I said.

Her eyes didn't track too well as she looked at me. She gulped in a lungful of air, which seemed to help. She focused and smiled at me. "Hi, E.J. Thanks for saving my life."

"You're welcome," I said, not being able to come up with anything better to say.

"Join us for some coffee, E.J.," Arthur boomed. "It's the least we can do. Hell, have a whole pot!" He laughed.

I was torn. Did I want to play Nancy Drew and go into these people's home and interrogate them? Interrogation never did seem to go too well with these two. Or did I want to stay as far away from them as possible? Curiosity won out over personal, physical, or mental safety.

I said, "Sure. I'd love some coffee."

Arthur beamed and Ginger smiled vacantly and they led me to the back door of their house, leaving their car in the driveway.

Ginger and I sat at the kitchen table while Arthur bustled about the kitchen, making coffee. Ginger said, "Why did you want to see me?"

"Excuse me?"

"The day you came over here and saved my life. Why did you want to see me?"

Oh, boy, I thought. Because I wanted to break your skinny neck because you were handy, I thought. Thinking quickly, I said, "Ah, I just wanted to tell you that Graham won't be in school for a few days. I thought you could let Conner know."

"Oh," she said. There was a long beat before she said, "Is he sick?"

"No. He and the girls have gone to visit their grandparents."

She smiled. "How nice," she said.

Didn't she realize it was the middle of a school year? Why wasn't she asking the obvious? Because she was so spaced out she didn't know what planet she was on, much less what time of year it was? Or because she already knew?

"So," I ventured, "how are you feeling?"

She smiled. "Fine, thank you."

"Well, I'm so glad you're better—"

"How did you get into my house?" she asked, the smile still on her face.

"Ah, I have a key. I'd forgotten about it. It was one the Lesters had given me. When I saw your car in the garage, I got worried—"

Arthur set steaming mugs of coffee in front of us. "Thank you, dear," Ginger said.

"Thanks," I said.

Arthur beamed and sat down with his own mug. "Well, isn't that just wonderful that you had a key to our house! That's just marvelous. Otherwise, you wouldn't have been able to get in and save Ginger's life!"

"Yes," Ginger said, smiling. "That's just wonderful."

"I wonder if I might ask you a question," I ventured. I didn't get far.

Arthur jumped up from the table, still beaming at me. "Well, doctor says little Ginger here needs to get a lot of rest," he said, pulling my chair out for me. He helped me up and walked me to the door. "Thanks so much for coming over, E.J. And thanks for saving Ginger's life. We really appreciate it! You're such a good neighbor!"

The door, like so many around Arthur McLemore, closed in my face.

It was close to three o'clock in the afternoon (I know because my school alarm went off, sending me into a blue funk) when I heard the truck outside in the driveway. I glanced out the breakfast room window. The truck wasn't in my driveway, but the

McLemores'. I couldn't help noticing the lettering on the side of the truck: Kinney's Locksmith. Well, there won't be anymore of that life-saving crap going on at the McLemores' house, I thought.

I knew I should be taking advantage of the time I had on my hands to outline my next novel, rearrange the picture albums (we have one full of Graham's baby pictures but Megan's baby pictures were still in a box; I wanted to incorporate Bessie's pictures we'd salvaged from her parents' home, making a book of all three children), or clean out closets. Something. But all I seemed to be able to do was lie on the couch and replay all the horrors that had been happening to us over and over in my mind. At least until four o'clock when I could turn on *Oprah* and listen to somebody else's horrors for a while.

I was as close to solving my problems now as I had been weeks ago; that is, nowhere. The McLemores were strange, that went without saying. But could they really be behind what had been going on? Why? That was the big thing. Why would they be doing this to me? Okay, maybe there was some reason, some sick perverted reason, to kill their adopted son. But there was no reason I could think of for harassing me.

Scenario: Brad had been doing everything up to his death: the glass-laced chocolate, the 911 calls, the smut on my computer, stealing my royalty check, the sex toys—all that. Arthur or Ginger knew it. In their anger at finding out what he had been doing, they accidently killed him. Then one or the other, or both of them, stuffed Brad's body in the backseat of my car. Then, to take suspicion off Brad, they continued the harassment to make it look like he hadn't been doing any of it.

I sat up. That was pretty good. Everything fit. Almost everything. Why had Ginger attempted suicide? That was easy: remorse over killing her adopted son.

Or maybe she didn't try to commit suicide! Maybe Arthur tried to kill her! Why else have a locksmith come over and change the locks? Because he doesn't want you wandering in his house any old time using his phone and saving his wife's life. I chided myself. Why was Arthur going to the motor lodge in the middle of the night? That answer didn't come to me.

Damn, I thought. I'd had ample opportunity to search their house for electronic gewgaws, and I'd blown it. Now I'd never get the chance, now that the locks had been changed.

Angel called around five o'clock. "Hey, E.J. Willis asked me to call. He and Doug have to go to an emergency meeting at Chemco. He won't be home 'til late. Sorry."

I sighed. "I have a feeling Mr. Dietz is going to be a pain in the butt."

"Going to be?" Angel said. "I think he's already there."

"Hey," I said. "You wanna go get a bite to eat and see a movie or something?"

"Sure. I don't have any plans for this evening."

"Great," I said. "How long are you going to be at the office? I can pick you up there or at your place—"

"Naw. The office is fine. I have some things to clear up. How about around five forty-five?"

"Sounds great," I said. "You pick the movie."

Angel picked a Sylvester Stallone, which I could have done without: I have to see enough of that type when Willis and I go to the movies—but I just grinned and bore it. Afterward, we decided to live it up and go to the old Codder Inn for dinner in the restaurant.

The food there is as high class as it gets in Codderville. They even have snails on the appetizer menu, and they're not even deep-fried. When I suggested the old Codder Inn, I'd told Angel it was my treat— I knew how much she made as my husband's secretary. She'd never had escargot, so I ordered that as an appetizer for us to share, and I ordered Steak Diane while Angel went for the duck à l'orange. Afterward, we settled back with decaf espresso and contemplated the dessert tray.

"I haven't eaten this much total in a month," Angel said, holding on to her stomach.

"You can use the calories. And I, of course, have to keep you company. It's a rotten job but somebody has to do it."

"Bread pudding with a hard sauce? What's a hard sauce?"

"Whiskey," I said, sipping at my espresso alternately with my third glass of wine.

"Ooo, amaretto cheesecake."

"Good choice," I said, happy to be teaching this obviously food-naive young woman how to really eat. "I'll take the chocolate death," I said.

The waiter (the *only* place in Codderville that has waiters instead of waitresses—I'm talking class joint here) nodded his agreement with our choices and went off to round them up. I sat back and suppressed a ladylike belch.

"So how are things going?" Angel asked. "How are the kids?"

"Don't ask. My parents have had to go on the run with them."

"What? What are you talking about?"

I told her about Mr. Metallica. "I'd like to get my hands on this sleaze," I said. "Wouldn't be much left of him. I can be vicious."

Angel giggled. "Can I watch?"

"You know what really pisses me off? I have no idea how long this is going to last! It could go on forever! How long am I supposed to hide my kids away? How long am I supposed to live in fear?"

Angel touched my hand with hers. "Why don't

you go stay with the kids, E.J.? This has got be killing
you, being away from them like this."

"I refuse to let the bastard win," I said. "If I run,
he wins."

"If you don't, your kids get raised by your
parents."

I sighed. The desserts came, and I engorged myself
with calories.

I dropped Angel off at the office building where
her car was and drove back toward Black Cat Ridge.
With the serendipity of spring, the sky was black
velvet dotted with diamonds. The air coming in my
partially opened window was fresh and cool, but not
the least bit cold. I knew in a month and a half you
wouldn't be able to step outside without the heat
blast knocking the air out of your lungs, but on a
night like this I could almost pretend it would always
be this way: beautiful, calm, and sexy.

I had just started a fantasy about luring Willis into
the backyard to have my way with him under the
stars when I stopped at the light on the highway at
the Black Cat Ridge Boulevard intersection. A black
Lexus pulled out onto the highway, heading away
from me and toward the motor lodge. I turned off
my blinker and, when the light turned green, followed the Lexus at a discreet distance.

When the Lexus passed the motor lodge, I began
to wonder if I was following someone other than
Arthur McLemore, but I kept going, more out of iner-
tia than common sense. When the car pulled up to
the gate at the Brethren retreat, I knew it had been
Arthur I'd been following all along.

I continued past, pulling up in my hidy-hole I'd
found the day Ginger had jumped up and down on
Brad's grave. I got out of my car, watching through
the fence as the Lexus passed the main building and
headed toward the cemetery. A late-night visit to

Brad's grave? He didn't seem that devoted a daddy. Before he got to the cemetery, the car turned into the parking lot across from the small chapel where Brad's service had been held. Arthur got out of the car and headed across Luke Road to the chapel.

I grabbed the opera glasses out of the glove compartment and scanned the area. The Lexus wasn't the only car in the parking lot. There was a small compact, Japanese maybe. Dark color, navy or black or maybe dark red. The parking lot wasn't well lit and it was hard to distinguish.

What wasn't hard to distinguish was the little red sports car with the black ragtop coming down Luke Road from the guard station and pulling onto the verge next to the entrance to the chapel. The driver's side door opened and a man got out, closed the door quietly, and walked from tree to tree toward the chapel.

That's when I tested my high school calisthenic classes and scaled the fence into the Brethren compound. I lost my balance at the top of the fence and fell, knocking the breath out of me. I lay on the bluebonnet-covered ground for a moment, trying to catch my breath. My stomach was doing backflips and my breath was coming in short gasps. When I realized it had more to do with excitement than with the fall from the fence, I roused myself and moved stealthily toward the chapel. It was about a quarter of a mile from the fence to the parking lot. I covered it in short bursts of speed followed by tree-hugging breaks to see if anyone had been alerted to my presence. In the still of the night, I could hear a Christian radio station blaring from the guard shack. It took about ten minutes to make my way to the chapel.

Hugging the wall, I went around the building, trying to remember if I'd seen a back entrance to the chapel. I couldn't remember one, but I found it nonetheless. The door was unlocked and I slipped inside into total darkness.

The night, though moonless, was bright with stars, not to mention the occasional security light of the compound. The inside of the chapel, where I was, was totally black. I took a tentative step and stumbled. Righting myself, I realized I'd found stairs going up. After three steps I saw light above me and heard voices. The light enabled me to recognize where I was. Being a Methodist, it took a minute for me to realize I was in the baptismal font behind the chancel. The font was about waist deep. I squatted inside, peeking my nose up to the rim to see over.

Arthur McLemore was standing by the communion rails, holding a woman in his arms. Okay, so it was just a lousy affair after all. Then a door on the side opened and the man I'd seen in the red sports car came quietly out. Arthur and his lady love didn't see the man until he said, "I thought you had better taste than this, Sissy."

Arthur and the woman—Sissy—whirled around. The newcomer I could now see was holding a shiny, rather deadly-looking gun, pointed at approximately Arthur McLemore's privates. I could also see he wasn't Doug Kingsley.

"Bubba, what are you doing here?" the woman asked, clutching her hand to her bosom like one of my heroines might (okay, have often done).

"Followed you. Been following you for weeks, you bitch."

"Don't blaspheme in the house of the Lord, Bubba. You know that's not right," Sissy said.

"Ah, Bubba," Arthur said, his voice booming in the quiet chapel, "now why don't we talk for a minute? No need for the gun, boy. Just put it down and let's—"

"Shut up, you turd. Just shut the hell up."

"Now, Bubba," Sissy said, "watch your language. Think where you are."

"I can't cuss in the house of the Lord—but you can commit adultery here?"

Sissy's hands went to her hips. Her stance—I could only see her from the back—seemed indignant. "Why, Bubba Stimmons, I was doing no such thing! Me and Arthur just came here to talk!"

"You were kissing him!" Bubba shouted.

"Well, yes, but that's not committing adultery, Bubba, for heaven's sake."

The gun had been going back and forth, pointed at whichever person Bubba was speaking to. Now it was aimed again at Arthur.

"You killed my boy and now you want my woman," he said. "Well, that's just not gonna happen, Mr. Smarty-Pants McLemore."

"Now wait a minute, Bubba. You know I had nothing to do with Brad's death. It was that woman next door to us. She's the one you need to see about that!"

Well, thanks bunches, Arthur, I thought.

"Arthur would never hurt a hair on Brad's head. How could he? He's—" Sissy stopped speaking and turned toward Arthur. In profile, I could see she was biting her lips. "Oops," she said quietly.

Arthur grapped her arm and whispered, "Shut up."

"What?" Bubba said. "What's going on? Sissy, what were you about to say?"

"Ah, that, well, Arthur's a nice man's all, Bubba. He wouldn't hurt our baby. I mean, he took him in and all when we were just kids and too young to care for our baby, remember? Remember how grateful we were to him for that, Bubba?"

Bubba snorted. "Yeah, grateful, sure. He took my boy, then he killed him."

"Now, Bubba," Sissy said, stamping her foot. "He never! How could he hurt his own child?"

Behind me a voice said, "I knew it!"

Thirteen

I whirled around. Ginger McLemore was sitting on the top step, her feet dangling in the baptismal font. When I turned she lifted the gun sitting in her lap and pointed it at me.

"Come here," she said quietly.

I didn't move. She jumped into the font and grabbed me by the hair. There was another set of steps leading up to the chancel. Ginger dragged me up those. I was bigger than Ginger. I could have taken her. But the gun in her hand, shoved in my side, dissuaded me from any such thoughts. It took a minute for the bunch on the sanctuary floor— Bubba and Sissy and Arthur—to notice us up on the dais. When they did, Bubba said, "Well, shit."

"My sentiments exactly, Mr. Stimmons," Ginger said. "Looks like we've both been cuckolded."

"Do what?" Bubba asked.

"Cuckolded: make to look like fools." At Bubba's

dumber-than-dumb look, Ginger sighed. "Our
spouses have been messing around on us with each
other, Mr. Stimmons. And it seems to have been
going on for years, don't you think?"

"Yeah," Bubba said as light dawned. "It sure as
hell does."

"Now, Ginger—" Arthur started, but Ginger just
pointed the gun at him. Since Bubba was also pointing his gun at him, Arthur decided to shut up.

"Ginger," I said, "could you let go of my hair?"

"Oh," she said, turning to me and smiling politely.
"I'm sorry." She let go and I straightened up, rubbing my head. "But don't move, please, E.J. Or I'll
have to kill you."

"Okay," I said.

"Now, Miz McLemore—" Sissy started but Ginger
just waved the gun at her.

"You just shut up, you harlot," Ginger said.

"Now, just a minute," Bubba interjected. "That's
my wife you're talking to—"

I watched curiously as Bubba and Ginger pointed
their guns at each other. With any luck they'd shoot
each other and I could go home and get some sleep.

"Put down the gun, Mr. Stimmons," Ginger said.

"No, ma'am, you put your gun down," Bubba
countered.

"Bubba Stimmons, I was your Sunday school
teacher for three years, so you'd better listen to me."

The Brethren obviously ran a tight ship. Bubba
sighed and lay the gun down on the floor in front
of him.

"Thank you very much," Ginger said. "Now you
go stand with those two."

"I'd rather not, Miz McLemore," Bubba said, giving Arthur and Sissy nasty looks.

"Well, now I really don't care what you'd rather
or rather not do, Bubba Stimmons. But unless you

want me to start shooting off your toes, you'd best move." Ginger smiled sweetly.

Bubba moved over next to Arthur and Sissy. Sissy grabbed Bubba's arm. Bubba shrugged it off.

Ginger turned to me. "Now, E.J., would you please go join them?"

"Certainly," I said, and headed down the dais steps to the sanctuary floor below.

"Thanks for accusing me of killing Brad, Arthur," I said.

"That was meant in the nicest way possible, E.J.," Arthur said, smiling.

I let that one go.

"You killed my Braddie?" Sissy squeaked.

"No, I didn't—"

Sissy grabbed for my hair. She was a small woman, shorter than Ginger but with much bigger breasts. And she wasn't holding a gun. I grabbed her arm and twisted it. "Leave me alone," I said.

She squealed and tried to huddle up to Arthur, who moved discreetly away. Sissy wasn't doing well with the men in her life, and that was the truth.

I turned on Bubba. "Did you throw the Molotov cocktail at my house?" I asked.

"Naw. I just threw a bottle with some gasoline and a lit rag is all. I wasn't aiming for your house, ma'am," he said. "I was aiming at Mr. McLemore's house." He rubbed his shoulder. "My throwing arm's not what it was in high school."

Ignoring Bubba and me, Ginger said, "I should have known all along, Arthur. You always said not having babies was my fault. So to prove it, you slept with this little harlot and knocked her up, right, Arthur?"

"Ginger, honey—"

"And every time I mentioned adoption you were adamantly opposed. Then all of a sudden you want to adopt this bitch's bastard child."

"Ginger—"

"I should have known right then, but I was just too naive to think that you'd behave like that with a mere child, Arthur. That's truly tacky. I mean, her parents lived in a trailer park, for God's sake!"

"Now wait just a damned minute!" Sissy said, her hands on her hips and her foot stomping to beat the band. "There's nothing wrong with living in a trailer park—"

Ginger smiled sweetly. "Haven't gotten out yet, have you, dear?"

"Hey, now," Bubba interjected, his own indignation coming to the forefront. "We got us a nice doublewide—"

Sissy moved closer to Bubba and they united against this assault on their life-style.

"That really isn't the point, is it, Arthur?" Ginger asked.

"Now, honey—"

"The point is you brought your bastard child into our home and made me raise him."

"Did you kill Brad, Ginger?" I asked, keeping my voice conversational.

Ginger laughed. "Good heavens, why? That child was nothing to me. I had Conner." When she said her natural son's name, her face lit up. "My little angel. He's all mine. Arthur doesn't have a thing to do with him, do you, love? Not anymore than you had to do with your own bastard son."

My heart went out to poor Brad. He'd been doomed from conception. Conceived by an idiot girl and a selfish bombastic asshole like Arthur. Then brought home to be raised by Ginger, an unstable, also selfish woman with the warmth of a fudgesicle. The poor kid never had a chance. I was angry now, but for once I was angry for Brad.

"You people!" I said, hands on my own hips. "You

people are worthless, you really are! Have any of you ever thought about Brad? Ever?"

"I thought of Brad!" Sissy said, matching my stance. "He was my little boy and I knew Arthur could give him a better home than me and Bubba could." Sissy began to cry. "But now I wish we'd just kept him with us and raised him. I mean, we got that nice doublewide now, and two cars, and a VCR—"

"Well, hey," Bubba said, a quizzical look on his face, "he wasn't even my kid, right?"

He looked at everyone in turn, hoping somebody could explain this to him in words of one syllable or less.

I turned and started for the front door of the chapel.

"Where are you going, E.J?" Ginger called pleasantly behind me.

"Away from you people. If you want to start shooting, Ginger, go right ahead. But please start with your husband."

I walked out the doors of the chapel unmolested. And I didn't hear any gunshots after the door closed behind me. Not that I would have cared much one way or the other.

I got home to find a frantic Willis standing in the front yard, the cordless phone in his hand. "Damn it, E.J.!" he said, hanging up on whoever he'd been talking to. "Where have you been?"

I pulled the car on into the garage and shut off the motor. He was standing outside the garage doors glaring at me. "You won't believe me," I said, hitting the button to close the automatic doors.

"Try me."

"May I please go inside and get a cup of hot tea and sit down? If you don't mind?"

"Yeah, well, I do mind! You've had me scared half out of my mind! Do you know what time it is?"

"I have no idea," I said, walking in the back door.

"It's almost one o'clock in the morning!"

"So, when did you get home?"

"Hours ago! I've been frantic—"

"Honey," I said, sighing. "I'm sorry. I love you. I really do. I don't want to worry you. I should have called. Another good reason for a cellular phone."

I put the kettle on and got out the box of Sleepy Time. "Want some?"

"No—yeah—what the hell." He sighed and sank down into one of the kitchen chairs.

I bustled about, getting our tea, then set two steaming mugs at the table. I sat down and told him what had transpired that evening, from the Stallone movie to walking out the chapel door.

He started shaking his head when I told him about starting to follow the Lexus, and didn't stop, even after I'd walked out the chapel door.

"Jesus, E.J. Jesus. What did you think you were doing?"

I looked at him indignantly. After all, the answer to that was obvious. "Investigating," I said.

"Investigating what? What did you find out about what's been happening to us? Nothing, that's what. Just a wild goose chase that almost got you killed!"

"Do you think I should call the sheriff's office?" I asked.

Willis jumped up from the table. "You left those people with guns pointed everywhere and you didn't call the cops?"

"I just got home," I answered reasonably, "and besides, Ginger was the only one with a gun."

"Oh, for God's sake." Willis turned on the portable phone and dialed 911, telling them briefly that there was a woman holding people hostage at the chapel on the Brethren compound. When the 911 operator obviously asked who was reporting this, Willis said, "Billy Graham," and hung up.

At that point I started laughing. I was still laughing when Willis took me upstairs and put me to bed.

I woke up around ten. Willis was already gone, of course. I told myself not to get used to this luxury. My children would be home soon and there'd be no more sleeping late. From my lips to God's ears, I prayed.

I fixed myself a breakfast of coffee and Tootsie Rolls and contemplated what I'd learned the evening before. Not very damn much. I didn't think the McLemores had anything to do with what had been going on. They had their own problems and their own axes to grind that had nothing to do with me. I was just a meddlesome thorn in their side.

Was I back to square one? I'd gotten a good look at the little red sports car on my way out of the chapel the night before. It wasn't a Miata. It was an RX7. Both Mazdas. Slight resemblance, especially from the front, which was all I'd really seen of Bubba Stimmons's car. And Bubba had admitted to throwing the Molotov cocktail—excuse me, the bottle with the gasoline and the lit rag.

So that had nothing to do, apparently, with the other things that had been going on. My one real reason for suspecting Doug had been the little red sports car. Now I knew he had nothing to do with that. Then what about his behavior the night of the Chemco party? And what about the things he'd said the next day in my front yard?

Something wasn't right about Doug Kingsley. I slipped out of my nightgown, throwing on some jeans and a T-shirt, and drove to Willis's office. It was time I told Willis everything that had transpired with Doug Kingsley, and it was time Doug did some explaining.

*   *   *

It was close to eleven-thirty when I got to the Oak Hills Office Tower. Glancing quickly at the parking lot, I didn't see Doug's car. I said "Damn" to myself, making a woman walking past me look at me funny, and headed on up to the suite.

The door was locked when I got there. I had a key and used it to open the door. Willis wasn't there either. No one was.

I was alone in the office. Angel must have gone out to lunch. She wouldn't have gone much earlier than 11:30, so I probably had as much as an hour. But who knew where Doug and Willis were? If they were at Chemco, they could be gone ten minutes, or the rest of the day.

Doug didn't have an office in Willis's suite, but a desk had been set up for him in the big room, the room where the drawing boards and kitchen were. I moved quickly into the big room and sat down at Doug's desk, gingerly opening the drawers. The lap drawer contained pens, pencils, Exacto knives, rulers, and the like. The top side drawer held papers. Rifling through them, I saw printouts for the Chemco contract, bids on other contracts: nothing that interested me. The bottom drawer held a shaving kit, some Calvin Klein bikini underwear, cologne, deodorant, and a string of about thirty condoms: the kinds of things a stud like Doug would feel were important for those quickie dates right after work and no time to go home.

Behind Doug's desk was a two-drawer lateral filing cabinet. I'd have to talk to Willis about the security in his office; the filing cabinet, like Doug's desk, was unlocked. The top drawer held drawings of different sizes, lying flat in the drawer. The second drawer held more of the same on one side, the other side taken up with an electric pencil sharpener, drawing pens, more office equipment.

I stood up, stymied. I wasn't sure what I was looking for, just anything to implicate Doug somehow, some way. The two drawing boards were innocuous enough: one was empty, the other held a parts drawing.

The only other place to hide something in the big room was in the kitchen section. There were two drawers, a cabinet above the sink and a cabinet below. The first drawer held plastic knives, forks, and spoons, and a spatula that I'd been looking for at home. I put it on the counter. The second drawer held coffee filters and little packets of coffee, both caf and decaf, and a box of Lipton's tea. The cabinet above held coffee mugs and glasses, some Styrofoam, some glass, and my Tupperware pie caddie that I hadn't seen in months. I moved that to the cabinet top to take home with the spatula.

I moved to the bottom cabinet, squatting on my haunches in front of it. Inside were two extra coffee carafes, a brown-ringed one for regular and an orange-ringed one for decaf, a box containing more of the little coffee packets, two more boxes of tea, and hot chocolate packets. There was another box, smaller, with packets of instant soup. Behind these two boxes was another one. This box was black and didn't have the logo of the coffee service stenciled on the side as the other two had. I moved the boxes of kitchen supplies out of the way and slid the box to the floor in front of me. It was a smaller box than the other two, no more than one foot by one foot, no taller than six inches. The lid was as deep as the box, fitting securely all the way down. The box was made of heavy cardboard. I pulled the lid off. Inside was what looked like Willis's Norelco razor and a small black box.

"Know what that is?" a voice asked.

I fell back on my butt. Angel stood behind me. "Ah, I thought you were at lunch," I said.

She smiled. "No. In the bathroom."

I tried to get up off the floor. "Well, if you haven't gone to lunch yet, why don't you and I grab something to eat?"

"What were you doing snooping through my stuff?"

"Ah, Angel, I swear I wasn't snooping." I saw the Tupperware pie caddie sitting on the cabinet and picked it up. "I was looking for this," I said, smiling.

She smiled back. "Looks like you already found it. What are you doing with that box?"

I could feel my face getting red. It was really embarrassing being caught red-handed. Then the thought struck me: Why did she care? What was in that box?

I looked down at the black box, at the electric razor-looking thing and the little black box. "What is this stuff, Angel?"

She picked up the little black box. "This is what they call a blue box." She giggled. "But it's black, funny, huh? Anyway, it lets you dial any phone number you want. You just hook it up to any working phone, dial in the number you want the call credited to, then dial whatever number you want."

I didn't like the feeling I was getting in my gut. Stalling for time, I asked, "So—what? You use it for charging long-distance phone calls or something, Angel? That's awful." I laughed nervously.

"Yes, you can do that. Or make just about any call you want." She shook her head and laughed. "Now, this," she said, holding up the electric razor-looking object, "is actually called a laryngeal vibrator. It's for people who have had throat or vocal cord cancer. See?" She held it to her throat and turned a switch on the side of it. Then she said, in a singsong voice, "I know where the children are!" The voice was sexless, metallic.

I began backing up. Angel was between me and

the door. "Why?" I asked, stalling for time. Surely Doug and Willis would get here soon.

She cocked her head at me and smiled. "Why? You have Willis. I want him." She shrugged her shoulders as if to say, *"See how simple that is?"*

I charged her. I'd watched enough football on TV with Willis to know how to perform a fairly good tackle. And I had poundage on my side. Unfortunately, Angel knew the layout better than I did. She picked up a surveyor's tripod and swung. I suppose it must have connected.

My head hurt. I tasted something salty. I opened my eyes a slit. All I saw was the roof of a car. There were crayon marks on it. My car. I was in my car. Nice car.

I slid in and out of consciousness, the tire-on-pavement sound made me sleepy. I opened my eyes again when the car hit a bump, and another. I groaned, tried to sit up. It didn't work. I lay back down and closed my eyes. It was so much nicer with my eyes closed.

The car was stopped. The door by my head opened. I tried to turn my head and look but it hurt too much, so I closed my eyes. Rough hands pulling me. Falling. Hit the ground. Wet ground. I opened my eyes. I saw the sky. Bright. Too bright. I closed my eyes. My head hurt.

I was being dragged across grass and weeds. My arms were stretched back over my head and I could only see where I'd been, not where I was going.

My car was parked a few feet away from me, getting farther away as I was dragged. Behind my car I could see a dirt road, trees, grass. Swinging my head slightly to the left, I saw the banks of the Colorado River and the river itself. I seemed to be heading somewhat in that direction. My arms hurt, and my head. My butt hit a rock or something sharp on the ground. I moaned.

To my left was the old Brenham Road bridge. The road that had been replaced by the highway three miles upriver. Old Brenham Road wasn't used much. A perfect road to use when disposing of a soon-to-be-dead body.

Straightening my neck, I looked down at my body as it slid across the grass. There was blood on my T-shirt. My mind was so groggy I couldn't think straight, but I reasoned if there was blood on my T-shirt then, possibly, I was bleeding.

I jerked on one of my arms, freeing it from the grip that had been dragging me toward the river. My backward motion stopped. I jerked on my other arm but it didn't free itself as easily. I rolled my body toward the still captured arm, trying to twist out of the grasp.

Angel said, "Stop it, E.J." She laughed. "I shouldn't have let you eat so much last night. You weigh a ton." She grabbed for my free arm. I twisted and pulled away from her, freeing the other arm.

I rolled over, getting to my knees, trying to get up. Angel grabbed my hair, pulling my head back. The pain was too much. I fought to keep from blacking out again. When I felt a knife at my throat, I thought possibly blacking out might be preferable.

"I want this to look like an accident, E.J.," Angel said, "so stop messing around. Since you seem to be feeling so much better, why don't you just get up and walk?"

"If you want me, Angel, you're gonna have to work for it," I said. I lay down on my back and held up my arms.

"You're so silly," she said as she started dragging me again.

In our struggle I'd gotten a look at the riverbank. We still had about fifty yards to go. Therefore, I rea-

soned, I had fifty yards to figure out a way to save
myself. I was bigger than Angel, granted, by a lot.
But I was woozy. The knock on the head had disori-
ented me, and, besides, Angel had the knife. Maybe
I could have the knife, I thought. That would be nice
if I had the knife. I closed my eyes knowing that that
probably wasn't much of an idea.

I opened my eyes again when I heard an engine.
Coming up behind my car on the dirt road was a
little red sports car. Well, I thought, Bubba Stimmons.
Maybe he has his gun and he'll let me borrow it. I
closed my eyes and thought about chocolate.

I heard a door slam, then a voice. "Hey, Angel!
What the hell are you doing?"

I heard the pounding of feet and then my arms
were released and I was lying flat on my back on
the ground. I opened my eyes. Doug Kingsley was
standing in front of me. Angel was behind me. I
couldn't see her. I lifted a hand weakly and waved
my fingers at Doug. "Hi," I said.

"Jesus, E.J. You've got blood all over you—"

"She has a knife," I said. I think I said it—but I
might have thought it.

Then I heard Doug say, "Angel, what the hell? Put
the knife down, okay?"

Doug was backing up. Angel was stepping around
my body, moving toward him. I saw the knife glint-
ing from the sun. Then she lunged at Doug.

I heard him scream and saw him fall. I could still
see Angel's legs in front of me. I rolled over and
grabbed them, tumbling her to the ground.

"You saved my life," I said.
"No, you saved my life," he said.
"No, you saved my life," I said.
"No, really, you saved—"
"Oh, shut up!" Willis and Luna said in unison.
I was high as a kite. I hadn't felt this good since

1972. Doug, I presumed, had been given the same miracle drug I'd been given. We sat in our wheelchairs beaming at each other.

We were at Codder Memorial Hospital, in the emergency room. Doug had taken twenty-seven stitches in his shoulder. I'd gotten an ice pack for my head and was being watched for possible concussion. I'd also gotten some ointment for the grass burns on my butt where I'd been dragged by Angel.

When I'd knocked her down by grabbing her legs, Angel hadn't been ready to quit. But Doug had managed to get up and stand on the hand with the knife in it. After a minute, her fingers had loosened their grip and he'd been able to pick up the knife. I literally sat on her while Doug ran to the Miata to call 911. Sitting on her was about all I was up to at the moment. Luna showed up with the ambulance in about ten minutes. I'd used my T-shirt to stanch the bleeding on Doug's shoulder while he spent a great deal of time telling me what wonderful breasts I had.

Luna and a patrolman had taken Angel off screaming obscenities all the way. Doug and I had been packed away in the back of an ambulance and sent to the Codder Memorial.

On the way to the hospital, Doug told me that he and Willis had had a meeting at Chemco and had gone over in Doug's car. After the meeting, Doug asked Willis to join him for a cup of coffee and told him what had been going on between he (Doug) and I.

Doug had begun to get suspicious. Angel had been telling him on almost a daily basis about how wild I was and how Willis used me to get the Chemco account—my sexual favors with Mr. Dietz in exchange for the bid. And she also told him (something any man, much less a man as vain as Doug, would find very hard not to believe) that I'd been lusting after him since I'd set eyes on him, and told Angel all the time about all the nasty and wonderful things I wanted to do to him.

When Doug told Willis all this, and about Doug's come-on to me at the Chemco party and at our house the next day, Willis had gotten livid and had called a taxi to take him back to the office to confront Angel.

Doug left before Willis, getting to the parking lot of the Oak Hills Tower just as Angel was putting me in my car.

Concerned about my erratic movements and Angel's strange behavior, Doug had followed. The rest, as they say, is history.

Luna and Willis rolled Doug and me to the automatic doors of the emergency room entrance.

"Wait!" I said, grabbing Willis's arm.

"What, honey?" he asked, bending over me solicitiously.

"Can we get some of those drugs to go?" I asked.

Epilogue

The kids had been home for almost a month and I was wondering if my parents would like to take them for another vacation just as soon as school was out. Willis was in the backyard firing up the barbeque pit, and I was putting the last touches on my potato salad (Willis calls it Yankee potato salad because I don't use mustard, but I consider it merely the pure essence of potato salad: potatoes, mayo, chopped onion, chopped boiled egg, and celery seeds; it is the potato salad to beat all potato salads), when the doorbell rang. I wiped my hands on a kitchen towel and attempted to beat my children to the door. Forget it.

Graham opened the door to admit Luna and her sons, Luis, twelve, and Eduardo, fourteen. Both boys sulked in and agreed that it wouldn't be terrible to go upstairs with Graham. It wouldn't be great either, but they'd do it.

My girls followed the boys upstairs and started screaming when the door was slammed in their faces. I suggested they check on Bert (who was doing much better, by the way: he had hair on almost his entire body now) and (being in their nurse/nurturer phase), the girls readily agreed.

Luna and I went in the living room where Willis joined us.

"The stuff came in on Angel today," Luna said, "all the background checks we've been doing. And Willis," she said, looking at my husband, "do a better check on the next secretary you hire. It didn't take much to find out about this sick little chickie."

"So tell all," I said, settling back, knowing I would be doing the interviews for all secretarial help from now on. I was thinking of hiring Willis's mother. I wonder if she types?

"The first recorded event was in her senior year of high school in Houston. She stabbed a cheerleader in the leg from under the bleachers while the poor girl was running out onto the field. Seems the cheerleader was dating the captain of the football team. Angel wanted him. Her parents were able to get her put away in a private mental hospital for a while, in exchange for the charges being dropped. Father's a workaholic. Mother's into charity work. Only child. Kid was raised by a steady stream of illegal alien housekeepers, most of whom didn't speak English."

I glanced up the stairs, thinking of my kids. How would they turn out? What terrible things was I doing to their little psyches that would turn them either into mass murderers or Republicans?

"Anyway, she spent almost a year in the booby hatch, got her GED there, and then went to college. SMU. Decided she wanted her guidance counselor. Burned down his house after several months of harassment. The Dallas police never had enough to charge her with, and the counselor and his wife moved to another school in another state.

"Angel dropped out of college and went into the work force. Did you happen to notice how many jobs she's had, Willis?"

Willis sighed. "I pulled out her resumé when all this happened. She's only got three jobs listed, which is not unseemly for a twenty-eight-year-old. And, Luna, I checked her references. All her old bosses said she was a wonder. And she was."

"In more ways than one," I said.

"I mean," Willis said, giving me a look, "she was a good worker. Great skills. Typed ninety words a minute. Took shorthand at one-sixty. Knew the computer system."

"Especially how to work the modem," I interjected.

"Well, in reality," Luna said, "she had fourteen jobs in the past eight years. Sometimes she left on her own, sometimes she was fired for just being weird before anything happened, but in five cases, she was fired after she'd started harassing a boss's wife. Her last job? At a small electronics company in Houston. They built all sorts of spy-type electronics equipment. That's where she got all the stuff she used on you, E.J. But you were lucky. It looks like Houston is building a case of murder against her for the 'accidental' death of the owner's wife. She died while taking a bath with a hair dryer. Her husband kept insisting to the police that she wasn't that stupid. Now they're beginning to believe him."

"Did he suspect Angel?" I asked.

"I think so, although not enough to get her into what he thought was trouble," Luna said. "He did fire her, though, because he got tired of coming home and finding her in his bed after his wife died. He said he kicked her out of his house on at least a weekly basis."

"Jesus," Willis said, shaking his head. "Then I guess I was the one she was stalking, not E.J.?"

Luna nodded. "In a roundabout way. She's not talking, but the D.A.'s going with the theory that Brad, who we all know was a Peeping Tom, must have been staring at your house and saw Angel when she was messing with the telephone line. She killed him and left him in your wagon."

"Then who did what?" I asked, still not sure who to blame for each of the things that had happened to us.

"At this point, I think I can safely say that Brad stared at your house and messed with your jewelry. And that Bubba Stimmons threw the Molotov cocktail. Everything else we're laying on Angel."

"What do you think will happen to her?" Willis asked.

"She'll be charged here under the stalking law, and with Brad's murder, and E.J.'s and Doug's attempted murders. Also with breaking and entering and other lesser charges. When we're through with her, Houston wants her. Chances are, if she doesn't get the needle, she'll be in jail until she's too old to care about men."

Willis and I looked at each other. Neither he nor I believed in capital punishment, but when it got this close to home you had to wonder about your convictions.

"Oh, and Bubba Stimmons wants to make restitution on the damage to your backyard, in exchange, of course, for you not pressing charges."

Luna and I moved into the kitchen later while Willis went out back to check on the meat. Luna set the breakfast room table while I cut up vegetables for a tray.

Nodding her head toward the backyard, she asked, "So what's Willis going to do about Doug?"

I shrugged. "He's still pretty pissed. Says Doug

should have known what Angel was saying about our sexual life was a crock, and if Doug had come to Willis with it sooner, he might have saved everybody a lot of grief." I looked at Luna. "The thing is, a guy like Doug has to believe stuff like that about other people. Makes it easier to justify his own lifestyle."

"Is he going to stay on as a partner?" Luna asked.

"Through the Chemco contract anyway. His name's on that. I hope they can talk and work this out. But you know how men are: they aren't really big about telling feelings."

Luna laughed. "Now, if it was football—"

I laughed. "Oh," I said, "I have other news for you. Ginger McLemore's filed for divorce and is seeing a shrink, and it looks like Arthur's run off with Sissy Stimmons. And the house next door is, once again, on the market."

"I know," Luna said. "I put a bid in on it today." She grinned. "Howdy, neighbor."

It had been over a year since the Lester family had been murdered and Bessie had come to be part of our family. Now it was official. The paperwork had come: Bessie was ours. Our daughter. Legally and for always.

Bessie didn't go to the funeral of her birth family. She'd been too traumatized at the time, silenced by what she'd seen and heard that fateful night. Anne Comstock had suggested then that we not take Bessie to the funeral. That we wait. That someday she could have her own private service for her birth family with her new family.

Willis and I decided that afternoon, the afternoon that the adoption paperwork was signed, that it was time. Bessie knew and, I believe, understood that she was now officially a part of the Pugh family. We showed her the papers that listed her name as Elizabeth Lester Pugh. She was only five, and her reading skills weren't great, but she could read her name. Now she could read her new name.

The five of us, dressed in our Sunday best, drove to the Codderville Memorial Cemetery, parked the car, and walked hand in hand to the plot of land that was the final resting place of the Lester family. Bessie had never seen it. She walked from one grave to the other, looking at me to confirm who was where. I told her.

"This is Mama Terry. And here's Daddy Roy. This one is your big sister Monique, and the little one is your brother Aldon."

Bessie nodded her head. She let go of my hand and touched her mother's headstone, her little fingers tracing her mother's name.

"I can't remember what she looks like," Bessie said.

"We have pictures at home, honey. I'll show you." I knelt down beside her, putting my hands on her waist. "But I can tell you this: she was beautiful. She looked just like you. Your eyes, your hair, your smile."

Bessie showed me her smile. "Like that?"

"Just like that."

We all sat down on the grass at the foot of the graves and Bessie stood in front us, facing the graves of her birth family. In her clear, lilting voice, she said, "Now I lay me down to sleep, I pray the Lord my soul to keep. If I should die before I wake, I pray the Lord my soul to take."

After she'd finished, I pulled her to me and kissed her, then Megan, then Graham, who, in honor of the occasion, didn't wince. Then Willis, in his clear baritone, began to sing Terry's favorite hymn, "Amazing Grace." I said the words out loud, and the children would sing them, following Willis's lead.

The girls each had two bouquets of flowers that

they laid on the four graves. Graham had declined to participate in that part of the ritual. Instead, after the girls had laid the flowers, he stood up, reached into his pocket, and brought out a plastic figure I recognized as Leonardo, his favorite Teenage Mutant Ninja Turtle. Graham squatted beside Aldon's headstone and planted Leonardo's plastic feet firmly in the grass that covered the grave.

Standing, he said, "Now can we go to McDonald's?"